THE LAST THIRTEEN

BOOK THIRTEEN

JAMES PHELAN

Kane Miller
A DIVISION OF EDC PUBLISHING

7 BILLION LIVES ARE IN DANGER.
13 STRANGERS WITH TERRIFYING NIGHTMARES.
1 ENEMY WILL STOP AT NOTHING TO DESTROY US ALL.

MY NAME IS SAM.
I AM ONE OF THE LAST THIRTEEN.
OUR BATTLE ENDS NOW.

This one is for Leo, the little legend—JP.

First American Edition 2014
Kane Miller, A Division of EDC Publishing

Illustrations by Chad Mitchell. Design by Nicole Stofberg

First published by Scholastic Australia Pty Limited in 2014
This edition published under license from Scholastic Australia Pty Limited.

Cover photography: Blueprint © istockphoto.com/Adam Korzekwa; Parkour Tic-Tac © istockphoto.com/Willie B. Thomas; Climbing wall © istockphoto.com/microgen; Leonardo da Vinci (Sepia) © istockphoto.com/pictore; Gears © istockphoto.com/-Oxford-; Mechanical blueprint © istockphoto.com/teekid; Circuit board © istockphoto.com/Bjorn Meyer; Map © istockphoto.com/alengo; Grunge drawing © istockphoto.com/aleksandar velasevic; World map © istockphoto.com/Maksim Pasko; Internet © istockphoto.com/Andrey Prokhorov; Inside clock © istockphoto.com/LdF; Space galaxy © istockphoto.com/Sergii Tsololo; Sunset © istockphoto.com/Joakim Leroy; Blue flare © istockphoto.com/YouraPechkin; Global communication © istockphoto.com/chadive samanthakamani; Earth satellites © istockphoto.com/Alexey Popov; Girl portrait © istockphoto.com/peter zelei; Student & board © istockphoto.com/zhang bo; Young man serious © istockphoto.com/Jacob Wackerhausen; Portrait man © istockphoto.com/Alina Solovyova-Vincent; Sad expression © istockphoto.com/Shelly Perry; Content man © istockphoto.com/drbimages; Pensive man © istockphoto.com/Chuck Schmidt; Black and pink © istockphoto.com/blackwaterimages; Punk Girl © istockphoto.com/Kuzma; Woman escaping © Jose antonio Sanchez reyes/Photos.com; Young running man © Tatiana Belova/Photos.com; Gears clock © Jupiterimages/Photos.com; Young woman © Anomen/Photos.com; Explosions © Leigh Prather | Dreamstime.com; Landscape blueprints © Firebrandphotography | Dreamstime.com; Jump over wall © Ammentorp | Dreamstime.com; Mountains, CAN © Akadiusz Iwanicki | Dreamstime.com; Sphinx Bucegi © Adrian Nicolae | Dreamstime.com; Big mountains © Hoptrop | Dreamstime.com; Sunset mountains © Pklimenko | Dreamstime.com; Mountains lake © Janmika | Dreamstime.com; Blue night sky © Mack2happy | Dreamstime.com; Old writing © Empire331 | Dreamstime.com; Young man © Shuen Ho Wang | Dreamstime.com; Abstract cells © Sur | Dreamstime.com; Helicopter © Evren Kalinbacak | Dreamstime.com; Aeroplane © Rgbe | Dreamstime.com; Phrenology illustration © Mcarrel | Dreamstime.com; Abstract interior © Sur | Dreamstime.com; Papyrus © Cebreros | Dreamstime.com; Blue shades © Mohamed Osama | Dreamstime.com; Blue background © Matusciac | Dreamstime.com; Sphinx and Pyramid © Dan Breckwoldt | Dreamstime.com; Blue background2 © Cammeraydave | Dreamstime.com; Abstract shapes © Lisa Mckown | Dreamstime.com; Yellow Field © Simon Greig | Dreamstime.com; Blue background3 © Sergey Skrebnev | Dreamstime.com; Blue eye © Richard Thomas | Dreamstime.com; Abstract landscape © Crazy80frog | Dreamstime.com; Rameses II © Jose I. Soto | Dreamstime.com; Helicopter © Sculpies | Dreamstime.com; Vitruvian man © Cornelius20 | Dreamstime.com; Scarab beetle © Charon | Dreamstime.com; Eye of Horus © Charon | Dreamstime.com; Handsome male portrait © DigitalHand Studio/Shutterstock.com; Teen girl © CREATISTA/Shutterstock.com; Egypt pyramid © Roma74 | Dreamstime.com; Karnak columns, Luxor, Egypt © Mohamed Osama | Dreamstime.com; Egypt, Cairo © Ginasanders | Dreamstime.com, Egypt, Abu Simbel © Ginasanders | Dreamstime.com; Karnak temple in Egypt © Dan Breckwoldt | Dreamstime.com; Egypt, Luxor, Karnak temple © Ginasanders | Dreamstime.com; Old Egypt hieroglyphs © Swisshippo | Dreamstime.com; Karnak temple in Luxor. Egypt © Arsty | Dreamstime.com; Old map of Egypt © Ken Pilon | Dreamstime.com; Engineering drawing © Janaka Dharmasena | Dreamstime.com; Leonardo's engineering drawing © Janaka Dharmasena | Dreamstime.com; Leonardo's engineering drawing © Janaka Dharmasena | Dreamstime.com; Leonardo's engineering drawing © Janaka Dharmasena | Dreamstime.com; Antique carpentry wood workshop with old tools © Olivier Le Queinec | Dreamstime.com; Ancient workshop of a Luthier © Moreno Soppelsa | Dreamstime.com; Face Rameses II © Cunaplus | Dreamstime.com; Egyptian temple © Neil Harrison | Dreamstime.com; Aqueduct © Zaslavsky Oleg | Dreamstime.com; Aqueduct of Caesarea © Yehuda Bernstein | Dreamstime.com; Abydos temple © Rik Scott | Dreamstime.com; Sand pattern details © Larry Gevert | Dreamstime.com; Ancient scroll parchment © Guillermo Garcia Luaces | Dreamstime.com; Undersea ruins © istockphoto.com/LindaMarieB.
Internal photography: p26, Postcard © Mysontuna | Dreamstime.com; p59, Plaque © istock.com/rvbox, Vintage frame © satit_srihin/istockphoto.com; p73, Tablet © Jbk_photography | Dreamstime.com; p175, Anchorwoman © Alexander Podshivalov | Dreamstime.com, News logo © Rasà Messina Francesca | Dreamstime.com; p180, Folded newspaper © Capstoc/istockphoto.com.

For information contact:
Kane Miller, A Division of EDC Publishing
PO Box 470663
Tulsa, OK 74147-0663
www.kanemiller.com
www.edcpub.com
www.usbornebooksandmore.com

Library of Congress Control Number: 2013945973

Printed and bound in the United States of America
1 2 3 4 5 6 7 8 9 10
ISBN: 978-1-61067-284-9

PREVIOUSLY

Sam dreams of the next of the last 13, realizing it is none other than Alex. Sam wakes up trapped in a Melbourne hotel but is quickly reunited with Eva and Jabari. They travel to Antarctica to find Alex.

Alex manages to survive the harsh climate in Antarctica and is rescued by Hans and Dr. Kader. They continue their journey in Hans' mini sub, leading them to an amazing underwater discovery.

Xavier, Phoebe and the other members of the last 13 fly to Cairo to meet Xavier's father, Dr. Dark. But Dr. Dark seems strangely altered since they last saw him, raving about a map and an underground maze.

Sam and Lora, assisted by the Crawley base boss, Dr. Roberts, and his crew, set off in search of Alex. With a super storm forecast to hit in a few hours, their mission could not be more urgent. But out on the ice, Dr. Roberts is revealed as Stella in disguise. Sam barely escapes while Lora is taken prisoner.

Back at the base, Eva realizes the remaining crew are actually Stella's men and bravely fights them off to rescue the real crew. Banding together, they flee in snowcats, heading for another base and safety.

With the storm approaching fast, Sam finds a hut to shelter in, befriending two news reporters there. Refusing to wait, Sam makes for the Chilean base with an improvised ice sailer. But when he arrives, there's no one there.

Alex, Hans and Dr. Kader explore an astonishing cavern under the ice. There, in a pyramid, Alex finds his Gear. Stella tries to ambush them, but Hans blocks her path, while Sam joins them from the base above. Jabari appears and reveals he is still true to the Egyptian Guardians and will prevent the prophecy at all costs. The Professor makes an unexpected appearance and shoots Jabari. Hans' greed costs him his life, but the others escape to the world above.

Xavier becomes increasingly worried about his father's erratic behavior as they cautiously follow him into a hidden subterranean world. But Dr. Dark succeeds in discovering the maze. However, once inside, they get a nasty shock when Solaris reveals himself to be right there with them . . .

SAM'S NIGHTMARE

"I click my fingers," Solaris says, getting to his feet, "and all your friends die."

His black body armor is dull, no longer shimmering as though seen through a heat haze. But the menace in his voice remains as frightening as ever.

I gasp for breath, doubled over in agony. His shadow looms over me as he stands, prepared to resume the fight. I take a step back, struggling to get upright, and almost slide over the edge of the dusty stone surface. I glance backward over my shoulder, trying to see another way out. We are so high up, it seems as though thousands of rough stone steps cascade away beneath us.

I look down, searching for my friends. I can see them, standing in a circle at the base of this impossibly high pyramid. They look up, watching us.

Why aren't they climbing up? Why don't they help me?

But I catch sight of something else down there, shock coursing through me. It's a body, lying sprawled on the ground. I can't make out who it is.

Are they unconscious or . . . dead?

"See, Sam?" Solaris says, his sick humor evident in his voice. "Don't think I won't do it . . . again."

I turn to stare at the soulless black mask. "I'm not afraid of you," I whisper, my voice hoarse.

"Your Gears," Solaris says, with another, different edge to his voice now. "Give them to me. Don't play games with me, boy. Be thankful that I am giving you this chance."

I touch the straps of my backpack, feeling the weight of the precious Gears inside.

"And then what?" I ask, still defiant. "Then what will you do with us?"

"Oh, I don't know," Solaris says, walking around the top of the pyramid. I mirror his movements, keeping as much distance between us as I can. "Cold desert night like this, I could give you all a little . . . heat."

He shoots a stream of fire at the stone at my feet. I feel the unwelcome warmth running up my body. I force myself not to react, but I'm tense, frozen to the spot. I am overwhelmed by visions of all the fire that has ever scared me. I clench my fists and grit my teeth.

"Sam, Sam, Sam . . ." Solaris says. "Still frightened of a little fire?" He laughs.

Another jet shoots out, this time rushing by my head. I turn and duck. The heat flushes my neck. I open my eyes and in the early evening sky, I see the moon. It's full, its glow both beautiful and haunting.

"Are you really going to keep me waiting, boy?" he says.

I say nothing.

A kaleidoscope of images flashes through my mind—from another time, another place.

I'm dreaming, but is this really my dream? Is he manipulating the dream, manipulating me?

Solaris lunges at me and I move quickly, more easily now, keeping out of his way. I close my eyes and blink out the gritty sand that's been kicked up.

"You *are* dreaming, Sam," Solaris says. "You've managed to figure that out. But ask yourself—whose dream is this? Hmm? Maybe you should have stayed in school at the Academy a little longer . . . oh, that's right, you couldn't, could you?"

Again, I look down look at my friends, clustered around, barely visible in the dim light. I look at Solaris, standing there, his arm raised. The realization hits me suddenly, like a blow to the head.

I can't run any more. The race is ending.

"Maybe I did need to spend more time at the Academy," I say to him. "Or maybe I already know how to find out whose dream this is."

"Don't even try it!" Solaris says. "I'm in your head, boy, you don't stand a—"

I run hard, fast, right at his towering black form. I charge with my shoulder down low, just like my high school football coach taught me. Before he can react, I plow into Solaris' stomach and we go flying through the air—off the edge of the pyramid, out into darkness, falling through an empty sky.

I close my eyes and concentrate.

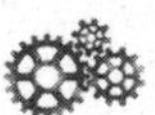

We hit the water hard.

I plunge down into the inky depths, my arms pushing out in front of me, my legs kicking fiercely to propel myself upward. When I reach the surface, my screaming lungs suck in air and I spit out the cool water as I look around.

It's night now. The moon is high and a handful of stars are sprinkled across the sky. I catch sight of a black shadow close to me in the water and I strike out for the shore, eager to put distance between us. I have caught Solaris by surprise with the sudden change in my dream but the advantage won't last long.

We're in a city—I can see buildings and streetlights surrounding us from above. I smile as I catch sight of the Eiffel Tower looming high over me, lit up against the night. To the right is the bridge where I'd landed on top of a tourist bus after Zara and I made our crazy BASE jump from the Tower.

This is my dream. I brought us here—to Paris.

"Argh!" I shout out as Solaris grabs hold, reaching out to me with impossibly long arms. His hand grips my backpack, dragging me to shore with long, powerful swim strokes. "Get off me!"

He's silent as he swims. I twist and turn, trying to pull against him, to swim in the opposite direction, but he's too strong for me. The backpack straps tighten as I struggle, I cannot get free.

Think . . . it's my dream, so I can control it.

Go somewhere else . . .

"Don't do it!" Solaris snarls, stopping to drag me around to face him, his voice still rasping and metallic through his mask.

I blink hard against the blinding daylight. I'm momentarily stunned by the heat in the air. Water pours off me as I scramble to my feet.

I've been here before, too—it's the Grand Canyon.

My last 13 tour, huh.

"You can't escape me," Solaris says. He's standing, facing me. He's still and menacing, yet I can tell he is impatient, all humor gone now as he chases me through *my* dream.

"Give me the Gears, Sam!" His voice is piercing, ripping into the very center of my mind. "You know that I will follow you, wherever you go. Paris, New York, Cairo, Arizona, Sydney—it doesn't matter. I'll be right there. And when you wake up? I'll be there, too. You have nowhere to go. There's nothing you can dream that I won't see. You've lost, Sam. It's time to give up."

He holds up something in his hand. It is a small, shiny silver disk—it glints in the sun as it spins gently on the end of a linked chain. It looks like an old pocket watch. Solaris is looking at it meaningfully. "It was made a long time ago. Now, it's mine."

"Nice story," I say. I scan the desolate scene around us.

If I can get away, lose him in my dream . . . then I can find the last Dreamer.

"You still don't understand what's going on here, do you Sam?" Solaris says. He takes a step forward, the antique timepiece in his hand. "Your destiny is my destiny, one way or the other, until this is finished."

Solaris turns to stare out at the expansive sky. Suddenly, everything changes. We are not in the desert anymore.

What the . . . ? I didn't do that.

But this is my dream.

Isn't it?

I stare, bewildered, at the rolling green hills around us, snowcapped mountains in the distance. I shiver and my breath swirls in front of me in the cold mountain air. We're standing at the top of a long valley, with a small, picturesque village nestled at the bottom of it, ringed by a dense forest.

"Maybe you don't know everything after all," Solaris sneers under the mask.

I gasp, the full realization of what's happening dawning on me. "But, if we're sharing a dream, like I did with the others . . . ?" My mind reels, grappling with an unthinkable possibility.

"That's right, Sam," Solaris whispers. "Do you understand now? The last 13 is complete."

No! It can't be.

But it is.

There is nothing now but the inescapable truth that our worst enemy is one of us. There can be no way to win this.

We are all going to—

Die.

SAM

Sam woke with a start, bathed in sweat, his heart beating like a drum. He looked across at his alarm clock—it was four in the morning. He'd been asleep for just a few hours but was *wide*-awake now. The long flight back from Antarctica the night before had both worn him out and messed with his body clock.

Sam climbed out of bed and opened the window, leaning against the old wooden frame. The chill predawn air washed over him, helping to calm his racing mind.

Outside, the London campus of the Academy was quiet. The grassy playing fields were deserted and an eerie fog was rolling in. Most of the buildings were cloaked in darkness.

Sam was briefly distracted by spotlights flickering in the small wood past the lake. The UN soldiers remained at their camp, still guarding the Academy walls, protecting them not only from Solaris, but also from the intense interest of the world. Beyond this protective barrier though, nothing else had changed. The leaders of the UN remained unsure and undecided about what to do with Sam and the other Dreamers, or about the race.

Don't they realize that they've nearly run out of time?

Sam took a deep breath in and tried to steady himself against the replay of his dream still running uncontrollably through his head.

The green hills, the mountains . . .

Solaris. He was in my dream—just him. No other Dreamer.

He *is the last one.*

Sam shook his head and pushed himself upright and away from the window. He paced the room with frantic, hurried steps. He wanted to pass it off as "just a dream," but he knew that it didn't work like that anymore. He'd known since the start that his destiny was inseparable from Solaris'.

But this . . . how could he *possibly be one of the last 13?*

What about the prophecy?

Sam shivered at the thought of what might be coming. Unable to process what was going through his head, he put on his Stealth Suit and boots and crept from his dorm room towards the staff wing, with one person in mind.

Lora.

As he passed paintings of great Dreamers—da Vinci, Tesla, Aristotle, Newton—he thought back to the first time he'd seen paintings like these, mosaic images made up of tiny portraits depicting the world's greatest Dreamers. He had been at the Swiss Academy then, seeing the pictures hanging impressively in the portrait gallery. At the end of the room were blank canvases, waiting, ready for future great Dreamers.

It was only for a second, but I saw myself, and Solaris, on a blank canvas. No one else could see it.

He climbed the stairs and walked by the teachers' rooms to the end of the hall framed by a large stained glass window catching the light of the moon. It was not quite full—not yet.

Light spilled out from under the last door in the corridor.

Lora's awake.

Sam knocked gently. He heard shuffling on the other side, then the door cracked open a little.

"Sam?" Lora said, opening the door further. She looked down the corridor behind Sam. Her face was weary. It was the look of someone who had lost so much—her boyfriend Sebastian, Tobias, students and countless Guardians—but underneath it all, Sam could see Lora's face was still resolute, she still held out hope.

Hope, in me.

"I . . . I think I just had my dream," Sam said. "My final dream, I mean. Number thirteen. But it's . . . confusing."

Lora nodded seriously. "OK, OK. Give me a minute, we'll go straight to the Professor."

Sam waited outside the door. There was a statue by the staircase that led up to the Professor's room on the next floor. It was a replica of Ramses the Great, copied from a temple in Egypt, Lora had told him.

All this—the Dream Gate, the Bakhu machine, the race—all started with him over three thousand years ago.

Sam sighed. They were so close to the end. So close to finishing what Ramses had started, on the brink of fulfilling the prophecy.

But how can my dream of Solaris be right? How are we meant to find the last Gear now?

"Ready?" Lora said, reappearing next to Sam and making him jump.

"Sure, yes. But, I was just thinking," Sam said, "do you think this guy was the first, like us, I mean?" He pointed at the statue of Ramses the Great.

"Yes and no," Lora said, following his gaze. They started to walk together down the corridor to the stairs. "He's certainly the first that we know about who spoke of the Dream Gate, and we know he was the one who hid it."

"And he created the prophecy?"

"That's right. But as for him being the first Dreamer, I wouldn't have thought so. I believe true Dreamers have existed for as long as there have been people."

Sam nodded slowly in agreement.

"History is like that, isn't it?" Lora mused. "We only know what we know from what we can put together in the jigsaw. But just because we can't find a few missing pieces, it doesn't mean they don't exist."

"Yeah, you're right," Sam said, walking up the stairs next to her and then down the small hall to the Professor's sleeping quarters. "Lora, maybe I'm wrong," he said, stopping suddenly, "about having my last 13 dream, I mean. I thought it might be the Gear—it seemed like it was. But it doesn't make sense. It can't fit. It *has* to be wrong."

"Wrong?" Lora said with a smile. "Sam, you know better than that. Trust your instincts."

"But maybe it was a trick . . ."

"A trick?"

Sam nodded.

Lora put an arm around him. "Come on, we'll soon find out."

As they approached the Professor's door, it creaked open. A tall figure stood there in the gloom.

"Sam," the Professor said, a dark-red robe swathed around him. "I had a feeling I'd be getting a visit from you."

"Professor," Sam said, "I think I had my next dream, well, my *last* dream."

The Professor looked to Lora. "We will need a dream machine, Lora."

"But—Professor, is that safe?" Lora said, pointing towards the window. "The UN is listening in on every electronic device in the Academy. Whatever we see, they'll see too."

"Jedi and Shiva have come up with a way to jam their frequencies," the Professor said. "And Jedi suggested we use an older device. Because the earlier models weren't wireless, it will be even safer from prying eyes. Besides, this is a risk we must now take, I'm afraid." He paused. "We don't have any time to waste."

"The moon," Sam said, looking out the window and suddenly understanding. "It's almost full. Just a day off, maybe." He turned to the others. "In my dream, it was full."

"A blue moon—" Lora said, now understanding the Professor's urgency too.

"Yes, Lora. The thirteenth full moon of the year," the Professor said.

"Blue moon?" Sam asked.

"The name for the extra full moon that sometimes occurs in a year," the Professor said. "If you have indeed had your final dream, we must act now. The full moon is tomorrow."

Lora snapped into action. "I'll get the dream machine."

"Thank you," the Professor said, and Lora ran down the hall, headed for Jedi's lab.

Lora returned faster than Sam could have imagined. Alex and Eva were with her, helping her carry the first-generation dream machine and helmets.

"What are you guys doing here?" Sam asked, happy to see them both. They looked awake and alert, like they'd already been up for hours.

"I found them in Jedi's lab," Lora said, setting up the

machine on the floor between Sam and the Professor.

"Jedi's gone to Amsterdam to meet Shiva so we were manning his den here. They're trying to contact Xavier and the others," Eva said with obvious worry in her voice.

"Still no word from everyone in Egypt?" the Professor asked.

"Nothing," Alex said. "All their phones are out. Seems most of the communications in and out of Egypt are kaput."

"That's probably why they haven't contacted us either, right?" Eva asked hopefully as she helped set up the helmets.

"I wish we could have gone straight to Cairo," Sam said.

"I understand, and I agree," the Professor said. "But Cairo is much more volatile than we had originally realized, and it was vital to give you a safe place to regroup and dream before the final race for the Dream Gate. I know it's frustrating but we'll be there soon." The Professor sat back in the armchair next to Sam. "All the more reason why we need to get moving here."

The Professor took a helmet from Lora, putting it on and sliding down the visor as Sam did the same. The wires connected them to a console between the chairs. Lora started adjusting the controls and dials.

"This dream was a bit different," Sam said to everyone, almost apologetically. He looked across to the Professor. "Solaris was there."

"But that's normal, isn't it?" Eva said.

Sam grimaced. "Yes, but this time, *he* had the Gear. He

said . . . see for yourself."

Lora paused, her brow creased as she looked at Sam, then to the Professor. The Professor gave a small nod and Lora plugged a screen into the dream machine so that they could all watch.

The Professor leaned further back into his chair. Sam saw the computer code whirring down the inside of his visor. The image blurred into pixelated colors, before focusing again into a scenic view of a clear blue sky over rolling green hills and majestic snowcapped mountains.

But this part of the dream wasn't mine . . .

ISSEY

"How much farther?" Zara asked. "Why is there no light ahead? Maybe we should have stayed with Dr. Dark and the others."

The flashlight in Issey's hand was dimming and he could feel Zara clutching him tighter as they walked back through the tunnels to Dr. Kader's workshop above.

"We are almost there now," Issey said. "It's OK, I think the door was closed, that's all."

He felt Zara sigh as relief flooded through her when the flashlight beam picked out the door ahead.

"See?" Issey smiled at her. "Let me open it, hold this." He passed the flashlight over and grasped the door handle with both hands, and was almost surprised at how easily it swung open at his touch.

They picked their way back through the basement levels, searching out the Agents that had stayed behind to guard the house.

"Hello?" Issey called out. They came out into a courtyard, deserted apart from a couple of birds sitting silently in the tree in the center, staring at them with beady eyes.

"Where are they all?" Zara said, pulling her jacket around her against the cold dawn air. "I thought they would be waiting up here for us."

"Come on, we'll go upstairs. Maybe they are resting," Issey said, but even he could hear the uncertainty in his voice.

Something is not right.

Spying a spiral staircase at the back of the courtyard, they went up to find a luxurious lounge area, full of embroidered day beds and palm trees in bronze pots, long white curtains swaying in the gentle breeze. It was eerily quiet. Issey turned to Zara, a finger to his lips. *Shh.*

Issey stepped forward silently with Zara, moving around the furniture, casting his eyes down the corridors that led off the main room.

Where are they?

He stopped abruptly as he bumped into Zara. She was gasping for breath, her arm outstretched, pointing to the floor to the right of them. As she made to scream, Issey clamped his hand firmly over her mouth, gently holding her as she turned away.

Two Agents lay on the floor.

Issey turned Zara's face to him. He could see the horror in her eyes. "We must be quiet," he whispered. "Please, can you do that for me?"

Zara nodded, tears streaming down her face as she forced herself to hold in her fear.

Issey bent down to the Agents, checking for a pulse, but there was no hope. Both had gunshot wounds that could not have been survived. He felt bile rise in his throat, shock and panic threatening to overwhelm him.

This is no computer game.

As Issey stood up, he noticed something amiss at the far end of the room. Potted plants were knocked over, furniture broken, with bullet holes in the walls and blood splattered at the bottom of a curtain. He caught sight of the other two Agents, also sprawled on the floor, gunned down protecting them.

They put up a fight.

They died for us.

We cannot let it be for nothing.

"What do we do?" Zara whispered to him, glancing around nervously.

"We find a phone," Issey whispered back. "We must reach someone, warn someone. They can send help."

They tiptoed down one of the corridors, gingerly pushing open doors, finding bedrooms and bathrooms, but no phone.

"Downstairs, I think," Issey said quietly to her. Zara started to follow him but there was a sound from a room at the end of the corridor.

A man coughing?

A door creaked open inside one of the rooms, footsteps moving across the floor.

Zara needed no encouragement, she was already frantically scurrying back towards the main room, Issey hot on her heels. They had almost made it to the lounge when a door opened behind them. Issey didn't stop to look, but he heard someone yell, "Hey! Stop, come back here!"

Nuh-uh!

Issey burst into the lounge, weaving through the furniture, Zara just in front, heading for the staircase. He caught up to her at the top and as they threw themselves down it, he turned to see two men in gray suits, guns in their hands.

Without a moment to lose, they sprinted across the courtyard, aiming for the front door ahead. Zara was wild-eyed next to him as he grabbed her hand.

A shot rang out from above them, splintering the plaster of the wall near Issey's head.

Uso!

They slammed into the door, the sound of people running towards them pounding in Issey's ears as they wrenched open the door.

Issey pushed Zara ahead of him onto the street outside. "*Go!*"

04

XAVIER

Xavier sat staring into the shadows. Maria, Poh, Cody and Rapha were huddled together. Phoebe paced back and forth, wearing out a track in the dust underfoot. Xavier looked over to his father, Dr. Dark. He sat awkwardly against the wall dozing, his head lolling back and forth.

He's really lost it, leading us down here—leading us to Solaris, like a fool.

Xavier grit his teeth.

When he wakes up, we're gonna have a tough talk.

Solaris and his heavies had gone, but they were still captive. He'd left motion-detection traps at either end of the tunnel which, if triggered, would release a wall of fire from devices on the floor. He knew that for sure. He'd seen it, tossing an empty water bottle through the sensor grid and watching it get roasted down to a melted mess.

Xavier had not closed his eyes beyond a blink. He was tired, but his mind was buzzing. He watched, he listened. Trapped, but not done.

Not like this.

There's gotta be another way out of here—we just have to find it.

They were under the pyramid complex, in the maze, the stone walls trapping them.

As long as Solaris leaves us down here, we're stuck.

So how do we beat him?

"I've had enough of this . . ." Xavier whispered to himself. He crept past his father and came close to one of the motion sensors. It looked like the sensor some stores had on their doors, making a buzz when the laser beam was broken by customers coming in.

But this was different, in two significant ways.

First, it wasn't just a single beam set at ankle height across a doorway. No, not even close. This projected beams in a crisscross pattern all over the tunnel opening, thin strings of red light from top to bottom.

The biggest space between the beams might be enough for a cat to jump through. Maybe.

The second difference was the canister attached to the device. It was a metal cylinder, about the size of a tin can. It had a "highly flammable" fire symbol on it. He swallowed hard as he looked closer, trying to make out if there was a switch or release or any way that he could get it off the sensor.

Nope, nothing.

There was only the dull glow of one flashlight between them. All the other batteries had run out. Xavier quietly moved to the other end of the tunnel. Same thing—same sensor, same canister.

Great, just great.

"Plotting our escape?" a voice said and Xavier nearly jumped out of his skin as he saw a tall shadow cast in front of him. He turned.

Cody stood there.

"Man," Xavier said, "you just scared the sand out of my hair."

"Sorry," Cody said.

The others got to their feet.

"How long has it been now?" Rapha asked.

"A few hours," Xavier said.

"Any sign of . . . ?" Cody began.

"Nope," Xavier said, looking beyond the red beams into the darkness. "Nothing."

They all looked at Dr. Dark, who was snoring quietly.

How can he be so relaxed at a time like this? And on that floor!

"Is he really sleeping?" Cody asked.

"Apparently."

No one said anything for a while.

What else is there to say?

Xavier silently watched his father. He couldn't work out whether to be angry, sad or both, at the fact that his father had led them down here, to *Solaris*.

"What is Solaris' plan? Why is he keeping us here?"

Maria asked finally. "What does this all mean?"

"It means," Xavier said, "that we're about to be on the wrong side of history."

"We gotta get out of here," Cody said.

"Easier said than done," Rapha said, looking again at the sensors.

"If Solaris comes back, we might have a chance," Cody said.

"How?" Poh asked.

"There's him and his two men, and six of us," Cody said. "Not counting your dad, Xavier, no offense."

"None taken, but this is Solaris we're talking about," Xavier said. "He's no slouch."

"He's right," Rapha said. "I heard he murdered the Guardians and Agents who tried to capture him."

"I'm afraid that's true," Xavier replied. "He's strong, he's fast and he's *ruthless*."

"Well, the Agents should be coming to look for us soon," Phoebe added, walking over to join them. "Zara and Issey have been up there for a while now. No doubt they're organizing a search party."

"I hope they don't take too long," Rapha said. "I am getting very, very hungry."

"That's not funny," Maria said.

"I know," Rapha said. "It *is* serious. And we only have one bottle of water left. We could die down here."

"Solaris isn't going to kill *us*, right?" Poh asked.

"He left us down here without food and water," Cody said, "so who knows? Maybe he *wants* us to starve or die of dehydration."

"Maybe," Xavier said. "But I doubt it. We're still of value to him."

"It's not like we are going to find more Gears," Maria said.

"But we need to be there at the end, remember the prophecy?" Xavier said.

"So what are we going to do?" Maria asked.

"Well, whatever it is," Xavier said, "we have to start doing it *now*."

THE LAST NIGHTMARE

Fields of swaying green grass fill the valley as far as I can see.

I am home.

A stream snakes down from the mountains and slices through the valley. Stone farmhouses dot the landscape. I pedal faster, towards town, racing down the hill. It's a patchwork of old stone and wooden buildings, housing the few thousand people who live in the shadow of the mountains.

I ride fast. Beyond the pines, I stop at a crest. It's uphill all the way from here. I drink cold water from a stream at the edge of the forest. The fading sun filters through the branches. I think about school. We have some tests next week, the final exams before I begin at the special high school where my father teaches. My father encourages me to study every night—not only that, he tests me, his teachings beyond anything we learn in class.

You are destined for something great.

That's what he's said to me since I can remember. He reads me books about the world's great thinkers—explorers, writers, artists, inventors—and tells me that, one day, I will *be among them*.

I start the uphill climb. At first, the bike's tires struggle against the dense and slippery pine needles that carpet the ground, but soon a narrow worn track emerges.

When I ask my mother about what my father says, about greatness and destiny, she says that she agrees. When I ask her more about it, she says that I must *follow my dreams*.

It's what she always writes on the notes she hides for me everywhere. It makes me smile.

Once I'm through the forest, the path winds down to a small waterfall. I stop to rest for a few minutes. I put the bike on the ground and take an apple from my pack. I sip cool water from the stream and eat. The sun is beginning to set. I know at this time of year, when I can no longer see the town bathed in sunlight, I have fifteen minutes of daylight left. I toss my apple core into the stream and watch it float away and disappear in the rushing water.

I ride the last section fast. I am on the school cycling team. We're good, although not as good as we could be. The others don't spend as much time training as me.

Why bother competing if it's not to win?

I can hear a low whirring noise above me, slowly getting louder. An aircraft? I look around. I can't see it. It gets louder still. I pull hard on the brakes and stop my bike. I look and listen.

WHOOSH!

It flies right over me. A helicopter, one that I've seen before. It's the rescue helicopter, from the city on the other side of the mountains. I watch it head down towards the town, flying fast. I'd love to fly like that. That's my dream—to one day be a pilot.

One day.

I smile as I take off again, riding as hard as I can up the climb, my legs burning, racing as though I could somehow catch up with the speeding aircraft. Its blinking lights disappear as it banks to the left, away from town.

There's nothing in that direction but farmland.

And our farmhouse.

Panic rises in my throat and I pedal harder.

My mind is racing and I am riding so hard that in the failing light I brake too late at the next bend and skid. My tires slide off the path and down the loose gravel that drops away into the gorge.

I bounce and tumble and crash. A small tree breaks my fall—without it, I would have continued on, right over the edge and into the ravine. But the collision also breaks my bike. The front wheel is bent so badly it can no longer spin. I leave it and scramble back up to the path and run towards home.

Towards my parents.

My father is a teacher—he works at a school across the mountains—and my mother is a writer. She also makes the local fleece into all kinds of amazing things. Once she wove me a dream catcher the size of my entire ceiling. My father pinned it up onto the wood boards.

At the top of the mountain pass, I catch my first glimpse of our house.

It's on fire.

The flames are *huge*, spiking into the sky—a giant pyramid of shimmering fire. Every part of the house is burning.

"No!" I scream as I run towards it. I can see two fire trucks are down at the final bend on the mountain pass, too big and heavy to get up the steep incline. The crews are running for the house.

The helicopter has landed nearby. I see my father, normally so tall, stooped and pacing back and forth in front of the house. He looks broken.

I know then what is happening, what the emergency is.

I reach the scene at the same time as the fire crew. They have air tanks on their backs and masks over their faces so that they can breathe despite the dense smoke. Some have axes in their hands, others carry extinguishers. They smash through the front door and rush inside. I run to follow them but the heat gets too intense. I hear my father calling my name.

I turn as he crashes into me and drags me back away from the inferno.

"Mama!" I shout.

"There is nothing you can do, son," my father says into my ear as he holds me.

"*Mama!*" I struggle against him but he clings tight, his strong arms wrapped around me.

"Shh . . ." he says. "Shh . . ."

Suddenly, firefighters burst out of the house. Fire and ash coat their suits and face masks. They are carrying someone.

My mother.

They rush her to the helicopter, where she is placed on a stretcher and wrapped in a shimmering silver blanket.

"Mama . . ."

"Here," she manages to say, looking at me. Her arm is outstretched. It's blackened and charred. I can't look at it. "Take it. And remember, dream big . . ."

I take the object from her hand and she is bundled

aboard. The door slams shut and the motor roars to life, my father dragging me away from the spinning blades. The helicopter lifts up into the sky and heads for the mountains, where it will take her to the other side, to the city.

Away from me.

I know, looking at my father's tearstained face, that I will never see my mother alive again. The heat of the fire is intense but we do not move. The firefighters stand there, helpless, with nothing to do but let the fire burn out against the night.

I open my hand. My mother has given me something precious to her, something that has been in her family for five hundred years. I clench it so tightly it hurts.

"Always remember what she said," my father says, his voice distant and quiet as a whisper. "Dream big, Sebastian."

POH

Dr. Dark snorted and shifted slightly. Phoebe reached over to shake him again.

"Pass me that water," Xavier said, crouched by his father.

"It's our last bottle," Maria said, handing it over.

"Yeah, I know," Xavier said, then undid the cap and poured a little into his hand. "I won't use much."

"Argh!" Dr. Dark said when the water sprinkled from Xavier's fingers hit his face. He sat upright, coughing.

"Dad—are you OK?" Xavier said. "You were sleeping, it was hard to wake you."

"Oh, I see, I'm sorry," Dr. Dark said, looking at Xavier, and at the others, and then at their tunnel prison, the realization hitting him all over again. "We're trapped down here?"

"Ah, yeah," Cody said. "Thanks to you, leading us straight to Solaris."

Dr. Dark said nothing. He looked from them to Xavier, and Poh could tell that he saw confusion, anger and disappointment on his son's face.

This is hard for him.

"Xavier, I'm sorry," Dr. Dark said. "I'm sorry, to *all* of you. I had no idea he was down here. I would never risk—"

"Regardless of how we ended up in this situation, it is what it is now," Phoebe said. "And we need to do something. We can't stay here."

"Right," Dr. Dark said, looking around. He scratched his head, his hair all messed up and full of sand and dirt, as was his bearded face and grimy clothing.

"Oh, great," Cody said, pacing away from them. "He's *still* nuts."

"Cody, cool it, man," Xavier said. "My father's not himself right now."

Dr. Dark picked up the water bottle and stared at the contents like it was something he'd never seen before.

"Yeah, well, I think he's going to wash his hair with the last of our water," Cody said. "At least we won't have to wait too long to die of thirst."

But Dr. Dark was looking at the clear plastic bottle, tilting it side to side, watching the water slosh around inside. Then he looked at the walls and floor around them. He touched the walls with one hand, the water bottle in the other. He reached up high, where there was a mark on the wall, up high near the top corner, which ran all the way down the walls.

"A watermark," Dr. Dark said, "where water once ran through."

Phoebe was watching him carefully now. Dr. Dark

moved towards the sensors. He was unsteady on his feet and the red grid loomed closer and closer.

"Dad, what are you doing?" Xavier asked.

Dr. Dark knelt down, eyeing up where the canister was attached to the wall beyond the sensor.

"Dad?" Xavier's anxiety was obvious to them all.

Poh watched as Dr. Dark took the water—and started to throw it towards the canister.

"Dr. Dark, no!" Poh said, rushing to him, fearing all their water would be wasted.

But it wasn't.

The water trickled over the circuits of the trap and it shorted out with a series of sparks and smoke. The grid disappeared. Poh grinned.

He is a clever man, Xavier's father.

"Genius!" Cody said, rushing over to Dr. Dark and helping him to his feet and clapping a hand on his back. "You're a genius! Forget all that other stuff I said, yeah? I take it back!"

Dr. Dark just nodded, then took a sip of what was left in the water bottle.

"Do you know where the tunnel leads?" Xavier asked him. "We came here from the other direction."

"No, I've never been this far into the maze," Dr. Dark said, tying his shoelaces. "But we don't really have a choice now, do we?"

"Right," Xavier said to him. "But—"

"Well, then, let's go," Dr. Dark said to them, his eyes clear and his expression resolute. "We've got a date with destiny!"

07

SAM

The stunned silence in the Professor's office felt as heavy as a stone.

Sebastian.

Sam took off his helmet, his hands shaking. He stared at the floor for a long time, too afraid to look up. No one spoke, no one moved.

Sam shut his eyes again and breathed slowly, trying to stay calm.

That was Sebastian.

Reluctantly, he opened his eyes and glanced over to the Professor. He was sitting there, motionless, his helmet still on, the visor covering his eyes.

"*He's* the final Dreamer?" he heard Eva whisper. "But how?"

"I don't understand—" Alex began to say, still standing alongside Eva where they had been watching the replay on the screen.

"Sam," Eva said, still whispering, "was that what you dreamed earlier?"

Sam shook his head, but still could not bring himself to speak.

"That was . . ." Alex mumbled, confused.

First, I dreamed Solaris had the final Gear.

That was Sebastian's dream. Sebastian had the same Gear.

No one spoke as long seconds ticked by.

"I'm . . . I'm not sure," Sam said finally, trying not to panic. He looked over to Lora, who stood frozen in the corner of the room. Her face was pale, her eyes unblinking. "Lora, I'm sorry . . ." he said. "I didn't mean—that was different from the dream that I remembered before. In the first dream, Solaris was there, in Egypt. We were fighting over the Gears. Then my dream jumped around . . . I mean, I did see that place, but not like *that*. We were in that field, but it looked a bit different. That house wasn't there. And the fire and . . ." Sam looked to the Professor, who was now slowly taking off his helmet. "That was *you*, wasn't it?" Sam asked him.

The Professor stood up and went to the fireplace. He leaned against the mantelpiece and looked into the embers, lost. Sam could see tears in his eyes.

"Yes, Sam, that was me, thirteen years ago," the Professor said, his voice sounding detached. Sam and the others waited in silence for him to continue.

When the Professor spoke again, it made Sam jump, his voice louder now, more direct. "I am sorry, Sam. There must have been a problem using this outdated technology—perhaps I took you into my subconscious, or recalled a memory from long ago. We can try again later, ask Jedi for a new dream reader." He turned to face those in the room. "You will find another Dreamer. I'm afraid this dream was not it."

"But," Lora said, checking the data from the dream machine, "that was *Sam's* dream, Professor, not yours."

"What?" The Professor's face was full of disbelief. "Impossible."

Lora tapped the machine. "This says that it was Sam's dream. We've just seen more of it than he recalled at first. Sam had to be sharing the dream with someone—with *him*." Lora looked distraught, now wide-eyed and breathing heavily.

"So that would mean that Sebastian isn't . . . ?" Eva's voice petered away to nothing as she gasped.

"I am sorry, Sam, but that dream *cannot* be. This was some kind of trick or you are mistaken. I'm sure you will have another dream that will reveal the true Dreamer. What you dreamed is . . . impossible," the Professor said. "My son is dead."

Sam looked to Eva and Alex, who looked as uncomfortable and confused as he felt.

"I'm sorry, Professor," Sam said, "but we can't just pretend this didn't happen."

"We all heard his name," Eva said carefully. "We all recognized who it was in the dream. We have to be able to talk about this, no matter how painful."

Sam turned to the Professor. "You've always told me

to believe in myself, believe in my dreams. This is what they've shown us."

"Hold on a minute," Alex said. "Are you saying what I think you're saying?" He glanced around the room, disbelievingly. "It's crazy, but it's true, isn't it?"

In that moment, Sam knew the truth for certain.

"Sebastian is still alive," he said. "Sebastian *is* Solaris."

"*Professor!*"

The Professor slumped forward, knocking over a small table as he crashed to the floor.

"Give him some air!" Lora commanded as she rushed to his side. "Get some water, quickly." She put a cushion under the Professor's head and cradled him tenderly, even as her own tears flooded down her cheeks.

They gathered around, Eva holding a glass of water, wobbling furiously as her hands shook. Alex put his arm around her, steadying her. Sam knelt down next to Lora.

The shock was too much.

He's found a son and lost a son, all in a moment.

The Professor's eyes fluttered open, his face ashen as he came to his senses.

Thank goodness.

"What happened?" the Professor said, struggling to sit up.

"Slowly, slowly does it," Lora cautioned. Sam brought him a chair and they eased him up into it. "You've had a shock—we've *all* had a shock."

"Yes . . . that's right, Sam's dream. No—*Sebastian's* dream . . ." the Professor said, letting out a sigh. "It cannot be, and yet, it must." He turned to Lora, their shared tears of relief mixed with bewilderment and horror. They embraced for a long moment, the only sound was Lora's sobs as she buried her face in the Professor's shoulder.

"He survived the crash in New York," Alex said quietly, voicing what they were all thinking.

"He must have," Lora said, wiping away her tears, forcing herself to regain her composure. "Somehow he survived and somehow he became . . ."

"Evil." The Professor stood up, wavering for only a moment, clutching at the mantelpiece to steady himself. "You are right, my young friends," he said, turning to Sam, Eva and Alex. "We must face the truth if we are to have any hope of winning the race. We must trust Sam's dreams and be strong if we are to prevail. There are so many unanswered questions, but we have to focus on what we must do."

"Professor, are you sure? Do you—Lora, need a moment?" Sam said, concern etched on his face.

"No, it's OK, Sam," Lora said, coming over to stand next to him. "Thank you, but we must deal with what this means now."

"But what *does* it mean?" Eva asked. "Does the watch Solar—Sebastian was holding contain a Gear?"

"That isn't a watch," Lora said.

"Lora is right," the Professor said. "It is an astrolabe—a type of early navigational tool, made in the 1500s. Sebastian," he visibly winced as he said his son's name out loud, "carried it with him everywhere after he lost his mother."

"So the Gear is inside it?" Alex said.

"It must be, which means it was either destroyed in the plane crash in New York," the Professor said, "or else Sebastian still has it in his possession. Either way, it is lost to us."

"But none of the Dreamers knew they were a part of the last 13 until Sam dreamed of them," Lora said, "so there might still be time to find it." There was a sudden clarity about the way she spoke, as though a revelation had hit her like a bolt of lightning.

"I don't understand," the Professor said to her.

Lora ran the footage back and stopped at the moment that Sebastian took the astrolabe from his mother's grasp. She zoomed in on the image.

"If that's got the thirteenth Gear inside it . . ." she said.

"Lora, what do you mean there might still be time?" Eva asked, confusion on everyone's faces.

"He gave it to me," she said, tapping on the screen, "a long time ago."

"He—he *gave* his mother's astrolabe to you?" the Professor said.

Lora nodded.

"Do you still have it?" Eva asked hopefully.

Lora shook her head with regret. "It was when we were still students, in our final year. We'd just started going out and we won the Dreamer Doors, which was held in Venice that year. That's how we won it, actually—we had the astrolabe with us and the final task involved navigation at sea, so it enabled us to take the lead."

"So—where is it?" Sam asked.

"The night we won the competition," Lora said, "we went to his family's crypt in Venice. In the middle of the night, we snuck in and left the astrolabe on his mother's tomb, as a tribute."

"But if that's true," Sam said, "then Solaris—I mean Sebastian—will know too, right?"

"Then we shall have to beat him to it." The Professor stared at the screen that showed the final image of Sebastian's dream. "We must act immediately." He turned to them. "Sam and I will go to Venice and retrieve the final Gear."

"What do we do?" Alex asked.

"Lora will take the rest of you to Egypt, to meet up with Dr. Dark and the others. You will find them there, nothing surer." The Professor nodded, looking around his office, mentally saying good-bye to it all. "And one more thing . . ."

They all turned to the Professor, apprehensive.

"You should call him Solaris. He's not my son anymore. *Sebastian* is dead."

ZARA

"This way!" Zara yelled, skidding on the cobbled streets. They ran out into the maze of alleys, flying around corners, turning randomly left and right in an effort to lose their pursuers. Gunshots shattered the early morning calm, a woman screaming out in shock as the gunmen gave chase.

Zara's legs were burning as they fled down a side street, narrowly missing a row of bicycles chained up in front of a row of small stores. Issey ran beside her, his tall, lean frame flying along in long strides.

More shots echoed out, shouts mingling with them, the chaos threatening to catch up to them.

Zara propelled herself on, turning to glance at Issey, pulling him on through an ancient archway. They ran past a small, ornate mosque. A door was ajar, an old woman sweeping the steps after morning prayer.

"We need to hide somewhere," Issey gasped. "We can't keep running."

He's right. We must ask for help.

Zara stopped, grabbing Issey's arm. "Follow me," she

said, retracing their steps to the front of the mosque The old woman looked up, her face creasing with concern at the sight of two teenage foreigners, gasping for breath.

"Help us, please," Zara entreated her, coming forward with her hands pressed together pleadingly. She cast her eyes back down the alley, empty for now.

They won't be far behind.

The old woman stared at them.

"Au secours, s'il vous plait!" Zara asked again. "Um, saa'adinii?" she tried.

The woman stepped forward, taking Zara's face gently in her hands. She searched her eyes for a long moment and nodded, smiling at them both. She turned to point at the mosque door.

"Merci, merci!" Zara gasped, sprinting up the steps with Issey. They dived through the open doorway.

The large circular room was cool but welcoming. A red-and-green carpet depicting archways filled the floor—a handful of worshippers kneeling among them. Above, rings of lights in glass holders cast a gentle glow. As Zara and Issey skirted further around the room, they stumbled over a collection of shoes.

Pulling their shoes off to add to the pile, Zara pointed to a plain office door on the far side of the church. A couple of locals turned to look at them. She smiled gently and pulled up the hood of her top to cover her head.

I hope this is not a mistake. I hope we have not risked these people's lives.

They padded quietly around the room, desperately trying to go unnoticed. Zara strained to hear any commotion outside. But there were no gunshots, no shouting, nothing that sounded like Stella's men had figured out where they were.

They reached the door, Issey cautiously pushing it open. It creaked as it swung, both of them cringing at the noise.

"This must be the imam's office," Zara whispered as they slipped inside.

"Yes, it is," a voice replied from within.

MARIA

Xavier was in front, using the fading flashlight beam to light the way as they moved as fast as they could through the labyrinth. Dr. Dark was next to him, Maria close behind. Each person had a hand on the shoulder of the one in front so as not to trip in the dark.

As they wound their way through the tunnels, Maria realized that there was a pattern to the maze. "We're headed towards something," she said, catching up to Xavier. "The floor seems to go lower, like we are always going a little downhill."

"That's right," Dr. Dark said. "We're heading inwards—there's been a long series of left-hand turns. We're getting closer to the center."

"The center of what?" Cody asked from behind.

"The Giza Plateau, so the pyramids, I should think," Dr. Dark said. "The water from the Nile was channeled through here. I understand that now, from seeing the waterline—it makes sense. It would siphon through the labyrinth. Perhaps it came through when the river flooded each year, or maybe year-round."

"Why?" Maria said. "Why would the pyramids need so much water under them? I mean, there was no one living in them. They were tombs for the dead, right?"

"I'm not entirely sure why, but I have my suspicions," Dr. Dark said. "Xavier, think back to what Ahmed told you about the pyramids."

"What?" Xavier said. "Oh, right." He turned to the others. "No mummies were found in the Great Pyramid."

"Really?" Cody said. "But aren't pyramids tombs?"

"Good question. *Are* they?" Dr. Dark said. "Were they? Where's the evidence?"

"Ahmed's theory," Xavier said to his friends as they continued on, "was that they were never built as or intended to be tombs. Think about it. Inside, these pyramids are plain and simple. No decorations, no intricate paintings or murals or carvings like the tombs in the Valley of the Kings. Nothing at all. They weren't built as glorifying tombs, they were built to be functional."

Dr. Dark said nothing, pressing onward, taking the next left, each hallway getting shorter and shorter.

We are getting to the middle. Dr. Dark is right.

What will we find there?

"But to serve what purpose?" Cody persisted.

Dr. Dark stopped and held out an arm to halt Xavier and the others.

"What is it?" Phoebe whispered from the back, where she was bringing up the rear guard.

"Listen . . ." Dr. Dark said.

They all fell silent. Maria strained to hear. There was just the slightest sound of . . . *what*?

"Air," Dr. Dark said. "It's air, a breeze."

Xavier nodded enthusiastically, turning to Maria.

It does sound like wind, like it's whistling through a crack.

"Where's the air going?" Xavier said.

No one answered.

"I can feel it," Rapha said, holding up his hand. "It's blowing past us. From our backs—it's being pulled ahead."

"It means there's an opening, and we're close to it," Cody said. "Right?"

They continued around the next bend, going even more slowly, the flashlight now just a dim glow against the deep black of the maze walls.

Around the next corner, they came across a steel ladder. Phoebe came to the front of the group, peering upward.

"Well, I guess we have to see where it takes us," she said, stepping onto the lowest rung to lead the climb.

The ladder took them up through a large hole in the stone ceiling which led to a stone platform, where another ladder had been set. They climbed up to the next level, into a room, old and worn with age. It was bright, illuminated by lights, with a generator humming in a far corner.

As they quietly gathered behind a stack of boxes, Maria spotted someone in the room. He was bringing crates in from another room nearby and setting them down in the center of the chamber. She turned to Xavier as he motioned for the others to take a look. Maria could see how pale he had gone, even in the faint light. She craned around to see what he was looking at.

Diablo!

They had found Solaris.

11

SAM

"This astrolabe," Sam said, eating through his third package of in-flight snacks out of sheer nervousness. "What does it do?"

"It's a measurement device," the Professor explained. "Astronomers used to use them to plot the sun, moon, the planets and the stars. Being able to work out locations by the stars was handy for being at sea, too, so navigators on ships would use them to calculate their position."

"And this one in particular?" Sam asked. "I mean, is there anything special about it?"

"Well, I know that it was made in Venice around five hundred years ago," the Professor replied. "And it had been in my wife's family ever since."

"Was it made by da Vinci?"

"Possibly, though I never heard that said, and it didn't have his maker's mark. But he may have had a hand in creating it," the Professor said. "Whatever the case, the Gear may have found its way inside, either by accident, or the gear mechanism was recycled—which happened all the time back then—or perhaps it was placed inside deliberately." The Professor sipped his coffee, the steam swirling into the air. "Who could have foreseen that this piece of our lives was destined to be a part of the prophecy? All this time, wondering who Solaris might be, when all along . . ."

Sam could see that the Professor was struggling with fierce emotions.

And I can't think of a single thing to say.

I still can't quite believe it myself. Sebastian, that proud, arrogant son of the Professor, has been our enemy right from the start.

How long had he been plotting against us?

And why? Why??

Why would he turn on the Professor, his own father?

As Sam looked at the Professor, he could see the same burning questions weighed heavily on his mind. Sam shifted around in his seat, wondering how he could steer the conversation elsewhere.

"So, was your wife a Dreamer too?" he began cautiously.

"Oh yes, and far, far better than me," the Professor said. "She was still studying for her doctorate when we were living near a small village outside Lucerne and I was teaching at the Academy. I was *sure* that she was destined to become the principal there, not me." He paused, as though it all suddenly made sense. "In a way, I took up the role so that her legacy could live on—I have tried hard, every day, to be the teacher and leader that she would have been."

"Because of the—the fire, at your house?"

"Yes. A freak accident. I was in town when the call came. I raced out there as soon as I could—but I was too late."

They were silent for a while. "I'm sorry," Sam said finally.

"Thank you, Sam," the Professor replied. "It is in the past now. I mourn her, as I mourn my son, but it has happened and we must carry on." He looked with heavy eyes at Sam.

They sat in silence, with just the hum of the engines to drown out their thoughts.

12

CODY

Cody could feel his heartbeat pounding in his ears. It felt so loud, he thought Solaris would hear it and discover them.

They crouched behind the boxes stacked near the top of the ladder, watching as Solaris marshalled the crates lying scattered on the floor, examining and checking all kinds of equipment. It looked like there was enough for a small army.

Awesome. As if Solaris wasn't enough on his own.

"We must be directly under the Great Pyramid," Phoebe whispered. "There are chambers underneath it."

"What do we do?" Xavier said. He turned to his father, who was blankly watching on, either puzzled by the sight or slipping back into some kind of sleepy trance.

"We move," Cody said. "We take him while we can."

"Huh?" Poh said. "Take him where?"

"No, we need to—" Phoebe said.

Gotta walk the talk!

Before anyone could say another word, Cody sprinted across the gap between them and another pile of boxes.

And then stopped dead, as though frozen. He stayed like that, like a statue.

"What is he *doing?!*" he heard Phoebe gasp behind him.

"I have no idea . . ." Xavier said. Then the others realized what had stopped Cody in his tracks. Another figure was now standing across the room. He too was working. He was tall, dressed head to toe in black body armor, with a mask.

Another Solaris?

"Que isso!" Rapha murmured.

"What the . . . ?" Cody saw another, and then another.

There's four, five—six of them. Six Solarises. Solari? Whatever.

They moved purposefully around the room, prepping for what seemed like an impending battle of epic proportions, organizing power lines from generators to set up work lights and more motion-sensing traps.

"Cody!" Maria whispered. He turned around. She gave an urgent wave. "Come back!"

Cody slowly made his way back to the others. They shrank into the shadows.

"You guys are seeing what I'm seeing, right?" Cody said.

"Think this is like a magic trick?" Maria said. "I mean, maybe they are holograms or something, no?"

"No," Xavier said. "They're as real as you and me—it's Solaris' men, just dressed up to look like him now. Who knows why—to trick us? To trick the others? We've just caught them out early. And we have to deal with them, surprise them, use that to our advantage before they're ready."

"Before they're ready for what?" Poh said.

"Maybe for when the others get here," Xavier said. "I mean, I bet this is to trick them, right? To fool Sam and the Professor, everyone."

They watched the Solaris army, transfixed.

"Who *are* they?" Maria said. "What terrible people would work for him and agree to dress up like this?"

"The world's full of people who'll do bad things for money," Phoebe said coldly. "Sometimes not even for that."

"In the meantime, the burning question is . . ." Cody said, "which one's the *real* Solaris?"

13

SAM

The water taxi was fast—the Professor made sure of it, with a generous tip to the driver, who pushed the boat to its limit and sped by all the other traffic on the waterway. Sam clung to the side rail. Water sprayed as they went airborne, smacking down on the waves created by the wake of other craft. They steered clear of the main canal system and skirted the old city, winding around to the other side of the Venetian Lagoon.

"Have you been out here before?" Sam yelled over the engines, the small polished wooden boat sweeping into a wide turn to get around a large barge ahead.

"A few times," the Professor replied. "We used to come here on vacation. But I've not been here since we buried Lucia."

"Where is the crypt?" Sam asked.

"Over there," the Professor said, pointing straight ahead to a low-lying island, "on Murano."

The crypt was near the center of the cemetery, part of a row of small stone buildings, each like a tiny castle that looked as old as the small island itself. As they approached, the Professor reached deep inside his jacket and pulled out two dart guns, handing one to Sam.

"We must be prepared," the Professor said. He tried opening the heavy, ornate door—it was locked and nothing short of a cannon blast would knock it down.

Built when people really knew how to build things.

"I'll go find someone who works here. Wait, I'll be back soon."

"OK," Sam said.

Sam waited nervously. The cemetery was immaculate, the grass neatly cut, all the headstones clean and shiny, made of marble and granite. Colorful flowers were in vases and terracotta pots. A few rows away, a handful of people knelt at the graves of loved ones.

Sam looked down. His shoes were scuffed and dusty. He noticed the small lump in the middle of his chest where the key hung under his Stealth Suit.

Then Sam looked behind him, at the crypt's door handle, and beneath it, the keyhole. There were *two* keyholes—one very different from the other.

No way.

He stepped away from the door, crouched down and looked closer. The first looked like a normal keyhole, but the second was very different.

"No!" Sam couldn't believe it. The shape was very distinctive. "I don't believe it."

He felt around his neck and took off the key that he'd found within the Star of Egypt sapphire.

It fit snugly into the second keyhole. He twisted it. The mechanism turned. There was a loud clunk and the door swung open.

Sam glanced around at the cemetery. There was no sign of the Professor. He stepped inside the crypt.

It was cold and dark inside. There was a small window way up high near the ceiling. It felt as though he was walking into a space that had been sealed up for years. There was a quiet hush and somberness to it.

"Probably *has* been locked up for years," he said to himself.

There was a small altar in the middle of the room, sculpted angels watching over the tombs. He went over to the wall to his left. Twelve plaques took up the wall, with space between them for what he imagined were coffins behind the panels. He looked at the dates. There were none more recent than the late 1700s. He went to the opposite wall.

Another twelve plaques. These dates went up to the early 1900s. The newer ones were different—the plaques had small brass trays, where people had left offerings. Some had stacks of faded old letters, others had coins and one held dried flowers that looked as though they'd disintegrate at the slightest touch.

Sam walked to the wall behind the altar, under the tiny window. More spaces, most with plaques, a couple yet to be filled. He found the most recent date, and next to it, a name.

Lucia.

On her offering tray was a little red velvet pouch with gold string tying it closed, covered in layers of dust.

Sam reached out to gently take the pouch in his hand. It was heavy. He could feel the object inside was circular and about the size of his palm. He looked behind him, to the open doorway, the sunlight spilling in. There was still no one there, no Professor. He undid the string on the pouch and tipped the contents into his hand. It was the silver astrolabe from his dream, exactly as he had seen it in Sebastian's twelve-year-old hand.

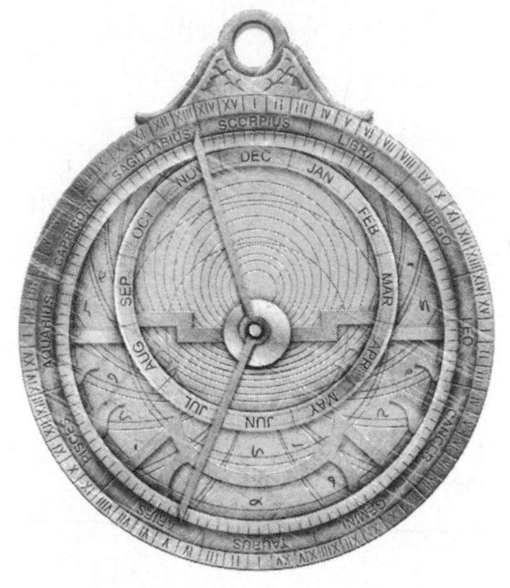

Sam looked up at the plaque. "Thank you, Lucia."

"That's it . . ."

Sam turned around. The Professor had come in and was looking over his shoulder. He was silent, his eyes going from the astrolabe to the plaque in front of Sam. He walked over to it and touched Lucia's name. He stood like that, still and silent, for two full minutes.

"Professor, I'm sorry, but we can't stay," Sam said.

"But, how did you get inside?" the Professor asked, facing Sam.

"I had one of the keys all along," Sam replied, patting his chest.

"Aha . . . it really *is* the key to it all," the Professor sighed.

"I don't want to rush you, but we should probably get out of here as soon as possible," Sam said, putting the astrolabe in his backpack and securing the straps.

"Yes—yes, of course," the Professor said, reluctant to leave, taking one last glance back at the plaque before turning away. As they walked past the altar, heading for the sunlight outside, a tall figure cast a shadow in the doorway.

Sam turned to the Professor just in time to see the shock and horror on his face before he fell, a dart sticking out from his neck.

14

Sam scrambled backward, hitting the far wall of the crypt with a thump as he fumbled for his dart gun. His fingers grasped the handle and he swung around to aim. But he was too slow. Solaris was on him, knocking the gun from his hand, slamming an arm into Sam's chest.

"Argh!" Sam doubled over in pain, but swept his left leg out to catch Solaris, pushing him over and leaping away to the other side of the room. He ran to the Professor, grabbing him around the collar, trying to drag him out.

No time.

Sam turned back to face Solaris, but remained standing protectively in front the Professor as he squared up to his enemy.

"Oh, how noble of you," Solaris mocked, "how *caring*. But it's too late for that. Far, *far* too late."

"How can you hurt him?" Sam yelled, his face hot with anger. "What did he ever do to you, *Sebastian?*"

Even though the mask hid his face, Sam was sure he saw Solaris flinch, just for a moment. "So now you think you know me, boy?"

"I know the Professor is your father," Sam said.

Solaris laughed, a long, heartless laugh that rang around the small stone chamber. "So?"

Sam's eyes flicked to the open door behind him.

Option one, run for it. Hope he won't hurt the Professor.

Sam looked down at the Professor sprawled unconscious on the floor.

Option two it is.

"I know you let him believe you were dead," Sam said, "let him grieve for you, his only son. I know you've turned your back on everything he ever taught you."

"You know *nothing!*"

Solaris charged towards him, his arms outstretched. But Sam was ready this time and moved out of the way with lightning speed.

Solaris crashed into the altar with a shuddering thump. "Seems you're getting faster," he muttered.

"Yeah, I am." Sam tumbled forward, rolling fast with a fist aimed at Solaris' chest.

Solaris dodged and came back with a strike of his own, a blow to the back.

"Argh!" Sam yelled out, struggling to his feet, turning to face Solaris, bringing up his fists.

"So, we could do this all day," Solaris said, "but this ends now. You're coming with me."

"You're crazy!" Sam spat out. "Why would I go anywhere with you?"

"Because of them," Solaris said, laughing as he pointed behind Sam.

Sam edged to the side wall to glance back without taking his focus from Solaris.

I'm not falling for the "look behind you" trick.

But it was no trick. Two men stood in the doorway, their guns pointed at Sam.

No!

"Think very carefully," Solaris said as Sam flattened himself against the wall, his eyes searching for a weapon, any weapon, to even up the fight. "I need you, but I don't need *him*." Solaris reached out a foot to nudge the Professor, still lying sprawled on the floor.

"You'd kill your own *father?*" Sam said, realizing the truth of the words as he spoke them. Solaris simply shrugged.

There's no hope for him now. Not if he can do that.

I can't risk it. I'll have to find another way.

"OK, fine," Sam muttered through clenched teeth. "But leave the Professor out of it."

"Oh, I don't think so," Solaris replied. "I'd hate for the old man to miss all the fun at the end."

One of the men came forward, wrenching Sam's backpack from him, poking him with the gun. "You walk now," he grunted.

Sam reluctantly stepped away from the Professor as the other man hauled him up and over his shoulder.

Outside, the sun was shining and Sam squinted against

the brightness, so at odds with the deadly situation. He was marched towards a helicopter, parked defiantly on a lawn in the middle of the cemetery. A groundsman ran up to them, waving his hands and protesting in Italian. But he stopped short at the sight of the armed men, turning to flee to the shelter of the crypts, where Sam could see other tourists cowering.

Solaris seemed not to notice, looking neither left nor right as they approached the helicopter. "Get in," he barked to Sam, swinging himself into the pilot's seat, motioning Sam to the rear.

Sam climbed in ahead of Solaris' men, who strapped him in tight, tying up the still unconscious Professor in the seat next to him.

"You won't get away with this," Sam said, almost to himself.

Solaris turned around in his seat as the rotors began to spin. "Oh, I think you'll find I already have," he laughed. "Enjoy the flight."

The man nearest to Sam leaned over, a thin smile on his face as the dart from his gun sunk into Sam's leg.

Sam felt a sense of helplessness wash over him as his world faded. The last thing he saw was Solaris taking the controls and the helicopter rising into the air.

15

ZARA

"I am Imam Fadil Abasi," the man said. "And you are?"

The man standing in front of them smiled warmly, no trace of concern in his voice. His face was covered by a wiry beard, his simple long black robes skimming the floor as he stood before them, an open book in his hands. The small office was crowded with full bookshelves, the early morning light casting its rays on them from a round window set high up above their heads.

Zara stepped forward. "We are so sorry to disturb you," she said, "but there are people looking for us, people who would . . . hurt us if they find us."

Do I tell him more? Say who we are?

She turned to see Issey flashing his red-carpet smile, trying to win over the old man. But his nerves were as shot as Zara's and his smile came out like a frightened grimace. There was a long pause as the imam considered them carefully. He closed the book, setting it down on the desk next to him.

"I believe you are telling the truth, child," he said. "Clearly, you have both been on a long journey. It must be time for you to rest and take shelter." He came forward, gesturing to them both to sit down in the chairs lining the office walls.

"You are very kind," Zara replied, letting out a long sigh, collapsing into the nearest chair. "We came back, and the Agents should have . . . but we were too late, and then he was firing and . . ." she choked on the words as she recalled the horrific scene at Dr. Kader's house and their desperate escape through the city.

What are we going to do?

How do we find the others?

Are they even still alive?

Issey sat down next to her, squeezing her shoulder. "It's OK, we're OK . . ."

The imam came beside them, crouching down to take their hands in his own. "I do not know your troubles, but you must stay here until we can make a new plan for you. It is dangerous now," he paused for a moment, "for Dreamers, yes?"

Zara startled and looked into his kind eyes.

Not all the world is against us.

"Thank you," Issey said, "we need all the help we can get. I don't suppose you have a phone? We need to make a very urgent call and this," he pulled out his mobile phone, "seems to be dead."

The imam stood up. "Of course, but we've had problems with our phones also. Cairo is in real trouble, but let us see what we can find. And then some food and time to clean up, I think."

Zara looked down at her dirty clothes and realized how hungry and tired she was. She felt light-headed as the thought of rest washed over her. "Thank you," she said quietly, sinking further into the chair. "Thank you." Zara also silently thanked her lucky stars that she took the chance to ask a stranger for help.

Maybe there's hope for the world still . . .

"We cannot stay any longer," Zara said. She saw Issey nod but knew he was just as anxious about leaving the safety of the mosque as she was.

They'd been there for hours, sleeping on couches in a back room, eating nourishing local food brought by the woman who'd been cleaning the steps earlier that day. The search for a functioning phone had been fruitless, Imam Abasi unable to find one that could make an international call. Even local calls were struggling to connect.

The imam told them that the city was becoming unhinged, the uncertainty of the race causing simmering tensions in the city to boil over. "You must be careful," he cautioned. "We need you to be safe so you can stop this madness."

He knows who we are.

As they made their way to the door of the mosque, Zara turned to grasp the imam's hands.

"I know," he said before she could even speak. "Go now. We will be praying for you."

Issey and Zara slipped out the door of the mosque, down the steps they'd raced up hours before. The city noise seemed even louder after the hush of the mosque. There was a nervous edge to the atmosphere as people rushed by, heads down and faces drawn.

They made their way back toward Dr. Kader's house, as they'd agreed, hoping to see that the others had come back or if anyone else had arrived.

Issey took Zara's hand as they walked through a thronging market just around the corner from Ahmed's workshop. They were surrounded on all sides by merchants selling their wares and customers bartering for the best deal.

Zara felt safer in this large crowd and wanted to linger there. She dreaded returning to the house where they'd found the slain Agents.

But where else can we go? How else will anyone find us?

She pushed on through the crowd, focusing on keeping Issey directly in front of her. But a man with a cart banged into her and she felt Issey's hand slip out of her grasp as she faltered in the square. Issey turned back, reaching out for her. But his mouth fell open in shock as he caught sight of something behind her.

Oh no!

Zara spun around, bringing up her arms defensively. She feared the worse. But she found something completely unexpected.

16

ISSEY

"Jedi!" Issey's shout could be heard even over the din of the market. He came forward to give him a high five, Zara still locked in a bear hug with him, tears of relief streaming down her face.

"And Shiva," Jedi laughed, stepping aside to reveal Shiva standing behind him.

"We . . . are . . . so happy," Zara sobbed, "to see . . . you."

"Hey, hey," Jedi said, "it's OK. We know what happened at Ahmed's house. But thank goodness the two of you managed to get away. We're going to stick together from now on, OK? We're tracking the others, don't worry."

"But—they were underground, with Dr. Dark and Phoebe," Issey said.

"We've gotten our tech working," Shiva explained, "and we've located the others."

"Come on, the director and Ahmed are arranging a jeep around the corner. Let's get out of here," Jedi said, leading them out of the marketplace.

A few streets away, they found the director and Ahmed

deep in conversation, standing next to a battered dark-blue four-wheel drive with dirty windows and a broken aerial.

"Zara! Issey!" the director called out as he saw them approach. "You're not with the others?"

"No, we came back because Zara needed a break," Issey said, "and then we found . . . at Dr. Kader's . . ."

"It's OK," Ahmed said, grasping Issey by the shoulder, "we have been to my house. Whoever attacked the Agents is long gone, there is no one there now. We will talk of this later, but we must go. Your friends need you to complete the prophecy."

They were bundled into the car, Ahmed behind the wheel, the director beside him. Jedi and Shiva cracked open laptops as Ahmed eased into the chaotic traffic, horns blasting all around.

"Where are we going?" Zara asked.

"Here," Jedi said, looking at a GPS marker on his screen. "Well, technically, inside *there*."

Zara and Issey craned to see the screen. They saw where he was pointing—at the Great Pyramid of Giza.

"They're *in* the pyramid?" Issey asked.

"Well," Jedi tapped the screen, "actually they're *under* it—about a hundred feet under it to be more precise."

"Look here," Shiva said. He pulled up schematics on his screen.

"There's a chamber down there, which was cut off from public viewing years ago."

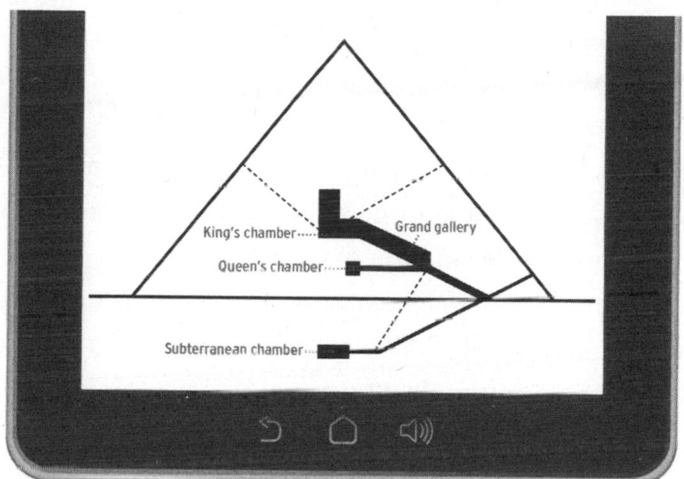

"What is it?" Issey asked. He clutched the side of the jeep as they bounced down the ancient streets. Ahmed threw the steering wheel this way and that, the car weaving through the crowded roads with impossible ease.

I should challenge Ahmed to a race one day.

"No one knows what the room was for," Shiva was saying.

"How do we get in there?" the director asked, turning in his seat to join the conversation.

"We can access the ascending chamber through there," Shiva said, pointing to the entrance. "But it's sealed off by a metal gate. There are more gates like that inside. The Egyptian authorities have not granted access to the chamber for a long time."

"You think maybe they're stuck down there?" Issey said.

"Could be," the director said. "With the prophecy about to be realized, the world is getting crazier by the minute." He looked out the window to the sun in the sky. "There are only a few hours to go." He turned back to talk to Ahmed, who was muttering as he tried to navigate around a broken-down car in front of them.

The engine groaned as Ahmed revved the car, edging out into the intersection. "Come on!" he yelled. "We have to—"

SMASH!

The jeep was flung sideways through the intersection as a truck slammed into them from the right, brakes screeching over the crunch of metal that filled the air. Issey felt the world collapse around him for an endless second before the car ground to a halt against a side-street wall. It was crumpled like a tin can, dust clouds billowing around them as the horn blared out in one long, angry scream.

Issey lay crouched on the floor of the car, Zara rolling over to meet his shocked gaze. A trickle of blood snaked down her face.

But she's in one piece.

We have to get out of here.

C'mon Iss, get up!

He unfolded his body, pushing back against the passenger door, which fell open when he kicked it. He pulled Zara by the arms, dragging her out into the street.

Jedi and Shiva appeared on the other side of the car, dazed but upright.

We're still alive, we're all OK.

But they weren't.

17

RAPHA

"Think of it as a game of chess," Phoebe whispered to the others. "We have to think several moves ahead to win. We lose our focus, it's all over. We have to stay calm and work as a team. OK?"

"OK," Rapha and Cody said in unison.

"Agreed," Xavier said. "And I *am* a champion at chess."

"OK," said Poh.

"Maria?" said Phoebe.

"Yes," Maria said slowly. "Solaris won't kill us, right?"

"No, remember, he needs us," Rapha said, looking at his friends with what he hoped was a convincing smile.

I know the prophecy says we all have to be there to open the Gate, but does Solaris believe it?

Rapha turned to look at Dr. Dark, who was crouched behind a crate, watching the masked men working away.

"But we have to try to escape," Xavier was saying. "And on the way, maybe we can make a difference, put a hole in Solaris' plans, whatever it is that they're setting up—"

"Some kind of trap?" Poh said.

"Yep," Xavier said. "So . . ."

“Just remember, these guys are armed,” Phoebe cautioned.

“But we have the element of surprise on our side,” Xavier said. “Isn’t it like what you said, a chess game that—”

“Shh, look,” Maria said. There was a commotion as the Solaris figures gathered together, their conversation too quiet to be overheard. Abruptly, they turned and left the room, heading out the main entrance, which could just be glimpsed around the corner. One figure remained.

“OK,” Xavier said. “Change of plans. We just have to get that one guy.”

“What if *that’s* the real Solaris?” Rapha said, looking at the man. He stood with his back to them, a dart gun in his hand, facing the doorway as though he was expecting trouble. “Even with all of us, we’re no match for him.”

“That’s not Solaris,” Dr. Dark said, watching him closely.

“You sure?” Xavier asked.

Dr. Dark nodded. Then—quicker than a heartbeat—he leaped out to rush the figure. He ran fast, but the distance was too far to make such an open attack and not expect to be heard on the approach.

If he’s going to have any chance, he’s going to need help!

“Plan B—scatter!” Xavier whispered to his friends and they ran to separate corners of the chamber, making as much noise and commotion as they could along the way. The guard spun in all directions, confused at their sudden appearance, not knowing where to fire first.

"Hey!" Rapha yelled to the Solaris figure. "Over here!"

The man flew around to face him, raising his dart gun just as Dr. Dark crash-tackled him from behind. The others rushed to help, pinning the Solaris figure down. Dr. Dark pulled off the mask to reveal an angry-looking young man. Fit and strong, Rapha thought, but nothing like the menacing threat he imagined Solaris to be.

"He's an Agent," Dr. Dark said. "A rogue, working with Stella."

"You'll never stop her!" the Agent said. "When she—"

WHACK!

Phoebe shot the guy with his own dart gun.

"Help me move him and tie him up," Phoebe said. "Arm yourself with whatever you can find in the crates. The rest of them might be coming back. We can barricade ourselves behind their equipment and take them out as they come in."

"No," Dr. Dark said, "no barricade. We hide this guy back near the ladder and we hide too."

"Then surprise them once they all come into the chamber?" Xavier said. "Nice thinking."

"OK," Phoebe said. "You heard him, let's do it."

"It pays to be a step ahead," Dr. Dark said as they picked up the unconscious Agent to move him out of sight.

"By the way, Dad, welcome back," Xavier smiled.

"Thanks," Dr. Dark said. "I have to admit, I feel much more like myself again."

“That’s good, because we need you,” Rapha said, Maria and Poh nodding in agreement behind him.

“Exactly,” Xavier said. “If we’re going to win, we need to be two steps ahead, and who do you think taught me to play chess?”

18

ZARA

Ahmed was slumped over the steering wheel, the horn still blaring as he lay there, unmoving. Zara and Issey pulled open the door as passers-by crowded around them, trying to offer help. Zara put her hand out to Dr. Kader's neck, searching for a pulse. But there was none. Steeling herself, she took him by the shoulders and gently pulled him back onto the seat.

We have to be sure.

She gasped and turned away. His jovial features were frozen in his last moment.

Dr. Kader's dead!

She felt Issey pull her around the car, and blindly followed him to the other side where Jedi and Shiva were tending to the director. He was laid out on the dusty ground, gasping for breath.

Shiva was bent over him, his arm cradling his head as the director whispered something to him. Jedi looked up, their shock mirrored in his face. "He's not going to . . ."

Shiva turned to them, his eyes watering. "I can't believe it, he's gone."

This can't be . . . I don't want to be here.

I can't do this.

"We have to go, *now*." Jedi stood up abruptly, pushing back the crowds surging around them and the battered car. "It's not safe here and we still have a job to do."

"Jedi, we can't leave them here," Issey said, wiping his own tears away with a shirt sleeve. "The police will be coming and—"

"Exactly," Shiva interrupted, getting up and brushing himself down. "And we can't be here when they arrive. Follow me."

"Are you out of your *mind*?" Issey yelled, now angrily pushing back against the people around him in his frustration. "Leave Dr. Kader and the director in the *street*? Run from the police?"

"We have no choice," Shiva said, grabbing Zara's arm and nodding to Jedi to follow him. "We can't afford to get entangled with the local authorities now. We have to leave them here, to go and fulfill the prophecy."

Zara shook her head. It was all too much to take in. The heat, the dust, people shouting on all sides, the small street full of noise.

And the director and Ahmed not with us anymore.

"Zara!" Jedi said. "Come on! You have to come with us, you too, Issey." Jedi started to pull them through the crowds, some of them pointing and becoming hostile at the sight of them leaving the crash.

"Wait!" Zara said. "What did the director say to you? Just now, before . . ."

Shiva sighed. "The last thing the director said . . . he said we have to beat Solaris. Like it or not, now you really do have to save the world."

Zara and Issey looked at each other.

"OK, lead the way," she said.

19

EVA

Eva looked out the window of the small Enterprise jet. They were flying over Spain. The sky was clear but for a few wispy white clouds against a bright-blue sky. Alex was asleep next to her. Arianna and Gabriella were talking together quietly in the seats behind. Lora slowly sipped her coffee, deep in thought, her eyes far away.

I bet I know what she's thinking about.

How must she feel about the fact that Sebastian is alive . . . and that he's Solaris?

Poor Lora.

The copilot came down the aisle from the cockpit, stopping to speak to Lora. Eva leaned over to hear what he was saying.

"We may have a problem," the copilot said.

"What is it?" Lora asked.

"I'm not convinced we're alone up here."

"Do you mean you think someone is following us?"

The pilot nodded.

"Who would that be?" she wondered aloud.

"Possibly the UN—maybe when they were watching the Academy back in London they realized someone had slipped out," he said. "Could be one of the countries alerted their air force."

"Hmm, so they're following us," Lora said. "They want to see where we go so they can inform their governments and have people on the ground when we get to the Dream Gate."

"So what do we do? Can we try to lose them?" Eva asked. Arianna and Gabriella were now crouched beside Eva, listening in.

"Depends what resources they have," the copilot replied. "If they can follow the plane in Stealth mode, they'll work out we're heading to the Cairo airport, I'm afraid."

"What if we land someplace else?" Lora said.

The pilot looked at her. "Where did you have in mind?"

"We can use the fact that Cairo is in such turmoil to our advantage," Lora said, "and break some rules. Take us to Cairo, as planned, but don't land at the airport, land at the pyramids instead."

The pilot looked at her in disbelief. Lora held his gaze. "Yes, ma'am," he said and turned to return to the flight deck.

"With any luck," Lora said, to Eva and the others, "we can land and disappear into the crowds before anyone following us can put together a ground team."

Eva looked out the window as the jet slowed and then came into a vertical hover. Below them were the pyramids of the Giza Plateau. Dense black smoke blew across the sky in gusty waves.

"That's coming from Cairo?" Eva asked, leaning over to look out the window. Alex moved closer for a better look. He whistled softly at the worrying sight below.

"Yes," Lora said, buckling into her seat for the landing.

"It's worse than I thought," Eva said.

Arianna and Gabriella were watching out their windows, too. They seemed too shocked to speak at all.

"Is it safe down there?" Eva asked as the aircraft started to shake around from the turbulence of the jet engines blasting against the ground. She could no longer see outside for the dust cloud.

"Nowhere is really safe anymore," Lora replied. "So stick close to me. Jedi messaged me a few hours ago and said they had Zara and Issey. He told me to meet him at the pyramids so we're saving time by going straight there. But we don't know where the others are. And we've possibly also got Egyptian security to deal with, so be prepared, OK?"

"Not going to be too pleased to have people land next to their pyramids, eh?" Alex said. "Let's hope the fact that we're trying to save the world keeps them happy."

Eva felt the jet touch down with a bump, then heard the engines spooling down. Lora unclipped her belt, then took a case from the overhead bin. She pulled out two dart guns and passed them to Arianna and Gabriella, then brought out two more for Eva and Alex. She pulled her own gun from its holster and checked it.

"Ready?" Lora asked them, as she readied herself to open the door.

"Ready," Eva said.

I hope we're ready.

The door hissed open. The stairs folded down and Lora rushed out first. Eva was close behind her, Alex and the others two steps back.

The five of them stood on the sand and looked around. There was nothing to see. The place was deserted apart from the pyramids that loomed over them. The air smelled of smoke. Gunfire crackled in the distance, and every now and then an explosion rang out.

"Well, that was a bit of a surprise," Arianna said. "I thought we'd be walking into chaos here."

"I am glad, though," Gabriella said, walking towards the Great Pyramid and looking up in wonder. "Wow . . ."

"The Egyptians must have already cleared the site and cordoned it off. With so much happening in the city, they've moved their security personnel there."

They moved away from the jet and watched it take off, heading to the airport to refuel and then return for them.

"What do we do now?" Eva asked once the dust had cleared.

"We wait for Jedi, and hopefully Dr. Dark and the rest of them," Lora said. "It's all we can do."

Eva nodded. A noise distracted her, a rustling of some kind and a muffled shout. Before she could wonder about it, a voice came out of nowhere.

"Now."

The five of them spun around but could see no one. Eva realized what was happening a split second after Lora.

Stealth Suits, set to blend in with the environment!

At that very moment, the threat made itself visible.

Solaris appeared between them and the pyramid. Then another, and another and two more.

What?!

Lora fired at the closest, Eva following her lead—the five of them firing at the Solaris figures until their dart guns were empty.

Nothing happened. The darts hit their armored suits and fell to the ground, useless.

"Are you done now, Lora?" one of the figures asked. It was shorter than the others, and took a step forward, putting a hand up to the mask to pull it back.

Stella.

Lora dropped her dart gun, flexing her fists, and moved in fast.

WHACK!

Lora smashed Stella to the ground.

"No," Stella said, holding up a hand and wiping blood from her nose. "I don't think so."

Stella turned to the men to her right and gave a nod. They bent down and pulled back a large blanket of Stealth material.

There lay Zara and Issey, Jedi and Shiva, all tied up with their mouths taped over. They looked wild-eyed and desperate, trying to scream out to them. One of Stella's men aimed a gun at them. It was clearly not a dart gun.

Stella's playing for keeps now.

"Your friends here were as careless with their security as you, Lora." Stella laughed as she got up, brushing off dust. "So, it seems that we are almost all here. This is becoming quite the party."

"Yeah, and who invited you?" Lora said to her, scowling.

Stella held Lora's gaze. "*Don't* tempt me," she said. "You are expendable, as are these other two." She motioned over her shoulder to Jedi and Shiva. "I'm just collecting the last 13."

"You'll never capture them all," Lora said. "So you might as well give up now."

Stella's face broke into a long, sly grin. "I think you'll find that Solaris already has your precious Sam and the Professor," she gloated. "Together with all your little friends we've got trapped underground, that gives us the full set. Game over, Lora."

Her cruel laugh reverberated off the stones around them, making Eva shiver.

SAM

Sam woke up just as the helicopter touched down. His eyelids fluttered, his mind struggling to come back into focus. Then the memory of their kidnapping from Venice came trickling back and he sat bolt upright and gasped for air. Turning, he found the Professor next to him. His wrists were tied together, just like Sam's.

"Where *are* we?" Sam said, peering outside.

"We're in Egypt," the Professor said. "Giza, to be precise. Solaris must believe, correctly I think, that Ramses took the Bakhu myth and used the pyramid to represent it in the prophecy."

"So you mean the machine needs to be assembled at the pyramid," Sam said.

The Professor nodded. "Perhaps at the—"

"Come on, you two," Solaris' henchmen growled at them from the open helicopter door, "out."

Sam got to his feet, stumbling a little as he climbed out and waited to help the Professor. He turned to see that Solaris had set the helicopter down behind the largest pyramid. Solaris knelt a little way off, his back to them.

"What's he doing?" Sam said.

"I suspect he's rifling through your backpack," the Professor said, "checking the Gears." He stared at Solaris, his eyes flickered with sadness, anger—a vast range of emotions.

So I guess they haven't spoken yet. How terrible for the Professor . . . but we have to stay focused. Focused on the race, the machine, the Gate.

Sam instinctively touched his chest where, under his Stealth Suit, the first Gear, the key he found inside the Star of Egypt, hung on a leather strap.

It's still there.

What will tonight bring, if the machine leads to the Dream Gate and Solaris opens it?

Will he have control over the Dreamscape, creating endless nightmares?

Or will it turn out to be like my first nightmare, the world burning, everyone burning . . .

He looked around. A tall fence stood in the distance, marking the perimeter of the Giza Plateau.

If I could make it to the fence, then the road—I could get to Cairo and disappear. The machine would be useless without my Gear.

Sam looked towards Cairo. Black smoke rose into the evening sky. The city was tearing itself apart—nightmares and chaos reigning.

"Don't even think about it, Sam," the Professor

whispered. "You'd never make it. You'd get twenty paces at most before they darted you."

"I can stop this though, can't I?" Sam said. "If I can get away with my Gear, the machine is incomplete—*it won't work*. I can still save us."

"No, Sam," the Professor said. "Take a look around you. The world is coming undone. The Gate *must* be opened, the imbalance has to be set right."

"But what if *he* controls it, then what?" Sam whispered desperately.

"We need to put the Bakhu machine together and see where that leads us. We will get a chance against him, I'm sure of it. We've come this far. We *will* prevail."

Sam nodded, trying to look more convinced than he felt.

And where's everyone else? I thought they were all meeting us here.

They watched Solaris put the astrolabe in the pack and sling it over his shoulder, walking back towards them. Sam felt the Professor bristle next to him, forcing himself to meet Solaris' fixed gaze.

"So . . ." Solaris said, "seems like my secret's out, eh, old man? How do you like your precious son now?"

"You're no son of mine," the Professor said through gritted teeth. "Not anymore. After everything you've done? All those innocent people you . . . I can't believe you could . . . why? Tell me, why? You owe me that."

"I owe you *nothing*," Solaris muttered, stepping closer to

the Professor for a moment. He turned on his heel, striding towards the Great Pyramid towering before them. He signaled to his men, "Holt, Pike, let's move it." They pushed Sam and the Professor forward. "Now, *climb!*"

ARIANNA

The group marched together through the entrance of the pyramid, prodded along by Stella's men. They headed along the descending passage. Lora, Eva and Alex were up front, tied together and following Stella, with Arianna, Zara, Jedi, Shiva, Gabriella and Issey in a second group behind.

"So what happened?" Arianna asked Zara out of the corner of her mouth.

"Dr. Dark took us underneath Dr. Kader's house, but I needed some air," Zara explained. "When we came back up . . . the Agents with us had been killed."

Arianna's shock was clear on her face, even in the gloom.

"There is more," Zara said, her eyes filling with tears. "We drove here, to the pyramids, but Dr. Kader and the director, they were hurt when our car crashed. They . . . they . . ."

Arianna stopped in her tracks.

No, I don't believe it!

How do we manage without them now?

"Move it!" the Agent grunted, shoving Arianna in the back.

She spun around, pushing angrily against their

captor. "You take your hands off me!"

Quick as a flash, the Agent slammed the butt of his gun into Arianna's side, making her double over onto the ground, Zara reaching out to grab her. "Keep moving, or there's more where that came from," he grunted.

Arianna exclaimed loudly in Russian, getting to her feet as Jedi came to put her arm around his shoulders, pulling her up.

"OK, OK, she's walking," he said. "Leave her alone." He muttered to himself, "You'll get yours, buddy."

"It's all right, I can walk," Arianna said, too proud to let Jedi help her for long. She held her side, trying not to wince too much. She turned back to Zara. "Tell me, where are Xavier and the others now? Where was Dr. Dark taking them?" she said.

"I'm not sure," Zara replied. "He had a map, he was talking about some maze he'd found. I'd never met him before but he was acting a little crazy."

"Stella said they were trapped down here," Arianna said. "I'm hoping that she is bluffing."

But something tells me this woman is not pretending.

They wound further down the passage, the corridor narrow and steep as it cut through the pyramid. Soon the surface of the walls changed, from the smooth and sharply-cut pyramid stones to rough rock face.

We must do something before they get us trapped underground.

As though reading her mind, Lora turned around and gave them all a meaningful look. It was a kind of "hang tight" look, one that Arianna had seen before on her missions with the Nyx. She hoped Lora had a plan.

They kept moving down the steep slope, lit by the Agents' flashlights, until they came to a very serious-looking steel door blocking their path. Stella pulled out a key and opened it swiftly, leading them through to a level hallway cut into the bedrock. As they went on, the space suddenly opened up around them. The subterranean chamber was full of crates and boxes, scattered around the room. There seemed nothing extraordinary about it, but Arianna felt the mood in the room shift. The Dreamers were all shoved into a tight group, the Agents with their guns up and ready, looking around.

But for what?

She could tell by Stella's face that something was wrong.

Arianna smiled.

Good.

XAVIER

"Shh!" Xavier said, running from the entrance of the descending passage into their chamber. "They're coming back, get ready!"

He and the others quietly readied at their positions. Phoebe, Rapha and Cody were nearest the entrance, hidden behind the crates that the Solaris crew had been unpacking. Maria and Poh were the next row back, hidden behind a high outcrop of rock that protruded into the center of the room. Xavier was hidden in the shadows, crouched in a carved-out niche to one side of the entrance. And his father was back at the hole that led there from the maze, ready to run out and create a distraction.

The first through the doorway into the chamber was a Solaris figure but the mask was off and Xavier recognized Stella immediately. She was followed by another Solaris—*what's left of her rogue Agents*. He waited for the other three to pass by, but got a shock at what he saw next.

It was Eva and the others, all of them tied together, first around their wrists and then from one person to the next via another rope. The other Agents brought up the rear.

It was too late to call off or change their plans. Xavier slowly came forward and made his move—sneaking up behind the last guy.

Two things happened at once.

First, Stella saw that the Agent guarding the chamber was missing and signaled to her crew while shifting all the captives to the center of the room.

The second thing was Dr. Dark. Xavier's appearance was the cue for his father to make *his* move.

Xavier could not believe his eyes. His father, who he'd known all his life to be impeccably groomed and wearing expensive tailored suits, looked like a madman. And not just any madman, but the president of madmen. And it wasn't that he only looked the part—he *played* the part too.

Dr. Dark came out running, screaming a battle cry, his eyes wide, swinging large wrenches he'd liberated from the crates in both hands. He charged at Stella like he was going to run right through her. In that moment, Xavier would have believed that his father could have taken on a brick wall.

But Xavier didn't have time to think about it, because he was grappling with the Agent he'd snuck up on. Sensing his presence, the guy had spun around and he was *huge*, easily the biggest of the rogue Agents. Xavier made to strike at the same time as the Agent, and was swiftly put into a headlock.

This isn't exactly going as planned.

Xavier grabbed at the arm around his neck, tugging at it, but it kept getting tighter. He was choking, and all his wriggling and squirming did nothing to shake off the Agent's grip. He started to feel light-headed as a vision of his friends jumping into the fray and his father attacking Stella swam before his eyes.

SAM

Sam thought he was dreaming. There they were—him, the Professor and Solaris—all climbing the Great Pyramid to put together the Bakhu machine that would show them the location of the Dream Gate.

Some dream . . . more like a nightmare.

He climbed up the last step of the pyramid, a place he had been before, right at the start of all this. He sat down on the stone and rested, his arms and legs and every joint burning from the climb.

This is where I first saw the key inside the Star of Egypt.

He looked down at the Professor scrambling up, still a few minutes from reaching the summit, one of Solaris' men behind him, prodding him onward. Solaris was on one knee, the contents of Sam's backpack spread out over the stone. The Gears glinted in the moonlight.

"Get over here," Solaris commanded.

Sam defiantly sat down where he was and watched Solaris trying to place the Gears in the right order. There was the Bakhu box itself that he had retrieved in France with Zara from da Vinci's workshop along with Zara's Gear, a crank-like handle. Then there were the other Gears, including Xavier's, which Sam had not seen since Solaris took it from them in Berlin. But every one was a memory for Sam—of each Dreamer and each country and how hard they had fought to win the race and get the Gears.

"You *will* do this, Sam," Solaris said, standing, pointing his weapon over the side of the pyramid—pointing it at the Professor. "I don't need him like I need you, *remember?*"

I'm so sick of his threats.

Sam silently got to his feet and went to the Gears. He sorted through the inscriptions on each, placing them in order on top of the Great Pyramid.

When will he realize that he's only got twelve here, including his Gear . . . that there's one missing?

The one that hangs around my neck.

"Put them into the box, do it!" Solaris said to him.

Sam started to place the Gears into the box in the order that they had found them. Each on a small crank shaft, connecting to the next.

After the third Gear, they didn't fit.

Wrong order.

"Why are you stopping?" Solaris jeered. "I thought you were the *one*, the key to the prophecy. Ha!"

"This isn't right," Sam said. He held out his hand to Solaris. "Let me try the last Gear first."

Solaris passed the astrolabe to Sam. He looked at it carefully, admiring the intricate craftsmanship.

So, how do I take it apart? How do I know which piece to use?

He turned it over in his hands, spotting a small but distinct "I" at the base of the back cover. Not immediately seeing any obvious way to open it, Sam turned his attention back to the Bakhu itself.

Maybe if I see where it's supposed to go, that will help.

He pored over the inside of the box with his flashlight, but there was no obvious position for the mechanism. Then he stopped. Looking at the outside of the box, he hesitated. He looked closer at the brass rings, holding the astrolabe next to them.

If this is how we read the location, maybe it goes on the outside?

Maybe the astrolabe itself *is the final Gear?*

Again he turned the astrolabe slowly in one hand, using the other to sweep across the face of the box, feeling the grooves with his fingertips. Moving it slowly, he very gently nudged the astrolabe across the surface of the Bakhu until it slotted quietly into place, in the middle of the rings.

Knew it!

"And the rest," Solaris mocked. "Don't feel too clever, you haven't finished it yet."

Sam scowled and tried to ignore Solaris' heavy stare as he turned his attention again to the Gears.

He took a deep breath and picked up Alex's Gear, the one they'd so recently found in Antarctica. Looking at the marked numeral "II" he knew he was right.

It's the reverse order, following the numerals.

Carefully, Sam put his hands inside the box, feeling around for where each Gear could fit into place. Long minutes ticked by as he fumbled with Alex's Gear. He heard the Professor arrive at the top of the pyramid, his breathing raspy, sitting down heavily to rest. Sam heard the Professor's sharp intake of breath as he watched Sam working on the Bakhu.

I bet he can't believe he's witnessing this.

Alex's Gear finally slipped into its position. Sam could

tell it was right as he moved on to Eva's small double Gears from Australia, searching out their place within da Vinci's mythical machine. They fit like they were made with modern precision engineering. On and on he went, back through the Gears found by Poh, Issey, Arianna and Cody. The inside of the machine began to take shape as each Gear's teeth clicked against one another in a perfect fit.

As he found the spot for Maria's Gear, Sam could see that once together, the crank handle could slot in the side of the box and set all the Gears, the machine itself, into motion. With every Gear he added, it became clearer how the machine might work—the toothed Gears would move as one, turning the astrolabe that would provide a reading on where they had to go. Set by the stars and the moon.

A full moon.

A *thirteenth* moon in the constellation of Ophiuchus.

Solaris came closer, overseeing the assembly and watching closely, ready to attack at any sign that Sam was stalling.

"That's it, boy," Solaris said.

Sam got to the eighth Gear, the one he'd found in Brazil with Rapha, when Solaris said, "Wait."

He crouched down close next to Sam. He looked at the machine, then the pieces laid out next to Sam's backpack.

He's counting them. He's about to realize that they're not all there—that we're one short.

What then?

Tell him a story? Tell him that the Gear is somewhere else—with Lora, or Alex or Eva?

Solaris looked at Sam. "Where is it?" he growled. He was still, waiting.

Sam swallowed hard. "Where's what?" he said.

Solaris said nothing. He stood, swiftly striding over to the Professor. He picked him up by his jacket and forced him backward until his feet were dangling off the edge of the pyramid.

"It's a long, painful fall from up here, boy!" Solaris said. "So what's it going to be?"

Sam hesitated. He never thought he'd be given a choice such as this, not so close to the end of things.

Do I lie, and hope to stall and save us all? Or tell the truth, and save the Professor now?

The Professor's hands grasped at Solaris' wrists while his legs were dangling and spinning in midair.

"The first Gear, Sam," Solaris said. "Where is it? I will not ask again!"

"It's here!" Sam said, standing, showing Solaris the key that was hidden away under his Suit. Sam slid the leather strap over his head and held out the key. "It's here. OK? This is the first Gear. The one I found in the Star of Egypt. The one that *Sebastian* died for!"

"No more stupid games . . ." Solaris said. He dumped the Professor roughly onto the stone. "Now, finish the machine!"

Sam looked to the Professor, who looked defeated, devastated by the knowledge that it was his very own son who was fighting against them. With each passing minute, the moon was getting higher in the sky. It had taken them a long time to climb up here, and the climb down would take nearly as long.

"Finish it!" Solaris commanded.

Sam crouched down again. He slotted the remaining Gears into each other, putting them in place so that the teeth of one would match up to the teeth of the next with a little metallic click.

All at once, Sam could see how the machine would line up the markings of the thirteenth zodiac to calculate where they needed to go from the points in the night sky.

All good, in theory. But will it really work?

And even if it does point to the Dream Gate—will it still be there, thousands of years on?

Can it really have been so well hidden that no one has discovered it?

Sam maneuvered Gabriella's Gear from the Pantheon in Rome, gingerly fitting it into the remaining space.

CLICK!

"That's it," Sam said. He stood, the machine at his feet between him and Solaris.

Solaris picked up the machine like it was as light as air. Sam noticed more detail of his suit now that he had time to take it in at close range. It was an exoskeleton, with black tubes that carried either air or hydraulic oil to black steel rods, levers and tiny motors. An exoskeleton, not just armor. It made him stronger, like he was half robot.

That's what makes him so strong and fast—it's not just a Stealth Suit, it's a mechanical suit. Is this the dreamflage suit that Mac said had been stolen?

"The key," Solaris said, effortlessly holding the machine in one hand and putting out his other to receive the first Gear in his open palm.

Reluctantly, Sam handed over the key and waited to see what would happen next.

24

ALEX

Everything was a blur as everyone moved at once. Alex felt the rope around his wrist fall away. He turned to see Rapha smiling at him, a small knife in his hands. Now free, Alex threw himself into the fight. But it was Eva who was winning it for them. In among the others, Eva was kicking butt. All her weeks of training were paying off in a flurry of movement—a kick here, a flip there, a block, a spin, a blow.

She moved like a whirlwind through the rogue Agents. Alex's mother and the others all hurled themselves at the Agents, catching them off guard and at close quarters. Alex saw Eva give a fierce kick to the one who had grabbed Xavier around the throat. Letting Xavier go, the Agent turned on her, but she was ready for him, jumping back as he swung at her.

Quickly overpowering the Agents with their greater numbers, Lora forced a dart gun from an Agent's hand and methodically darted the Agents, one by one.

"Thanks," Xavier gasped to Eva. "I started to go blue just then." He rubbed his neck gratefully.

"No problem," Eva said, looking at Stella's four unconscious rogue Agents on the floor.

"Nice work, Lora," Alex said, just as his mother rushed over to grab him in a tight hug. "I'm happy to see you too," he grinned, waving at Maria, Cody and the others he hadn't seen for so long. He pulled his mother away to see everyone now staring in one direction.

Stella had her back against the far wall, a dangerous look on her face, like a wild animal cornered.

Lora raised the dart gun to aim it at Stella. "I'm going to enjoy this."

"Coward!" Stella screamed, an ugly sneer on her face. "Just going to let it end like that? After everything . . . and I thought you were the great fighter." She spat on the floor in front of Lora, emphasizing her disgust.

Alex saw several people make to move forward, but Lora held up her hand. "Fine, let's do this, then." She handed the gun to a shocked Dr. Dark and squared up to Stella.

"I've been looking forward to this," Stella said, wiping blood from her nose.

"Lora," Alex said, coming up behind her, "you don't have anything to prove. Don't let her drag you down to her level."

"I'm not doing it for *her* sake," Lora said slowly, "I'm doing it for all the Guardians, loyal Agents, innocent bystanders *and* our students that she's hurt and killed."

"Oh, and don't forget your boyfriend," Stella sneered, "turns out he wasn't such a good guy after all, huh?"

Lora was silent, her face like thunder. She was in a fighting stance, ready to spring into action, ready to attack or defend in a split second. Stella circled around slowly to her left. Poh, Maria and Arianna moved out of the strike zone, everyone keeping tight together so she couldn't escape. All the while, Lora followed her moves and kept the distance between them.

She's waiting for Stella to make the first move. "Use your opponent's force against them."

Smart.

Stella broke first, charging towards Lora with brutal abandon.

Lora held her ground. She let Stella connect with a raised arm, and there was a brief grapple, then Lora leaned back, pulling Stella off balance, flipping her onto her back.

Stella rolled away and got to her feet.

Now Lora had a bloody nose too.

"How does that feel?" Stella said.

"Not as good as this is going to," Lora replied. She took three steps forward and feigned a kick, misdirecting Stella so she could throw her arm around Stella's neck from behind, dragging her in close. She kept the hold tight, squeezing. Stella tried to break free as they edged around the room.

"Lora!" Gabriella shouted out, but it was too late. Stella pushed Lora hard against an open crate, forcing Lora to let her go. Alex started to move forward as he saw Stella grab a crowbar from within the crate, swinging it menacingly at Lora.

"Here, take this!" Jedi tossed a wrench to Lora, the two women facing each other once more.

This is nuts, we have to stop it . . .

But it was too late. Stella threw herself at Lora, brandishing the metal bar. As the others scattered, Lora ducked under Stella's blow, bringing up the wrench to slam it into Stella's stomach. Stella stumbled backward, tripping on the uneven ground, banging her head on the corner of a crate with a sickening thud.

Stella fell instantly, crumpled on the floor in a heap.

Lora dropped to her knees, the wrench clattering to the ground.

Phoebe approached Stella cautiously with a dart gun in her hand, Shiva backing her up. "Everyone else stay back!" she ordered. She knelt down, searching for a pulse at Stella's neck.

In the silence, Phoebe turned to them and shook her head.

"Argh!" Lora sighed, partly in anger, partly in relief.

Stella's gone.

She's finally out of our lives—forever.

Alex tried to find some pity for her but after everything she had done, it was hard.

"You OK?" Eva asked Lora, bending down to help her to her feet.

Lora nodded. "I didn't mean to . . . I wasn't, but she kept coming at me," she said.

"She wouldn't give up any other way," Phoebe said. "It's done now. And my guess is that she would have captured you all, assembled the Bakhu and left us for dead down here."

"That's right," Alex said. He looked around, seeing the faces of the last 13 and their friends. "We should get topside, wait for Sam," he said. "It's time for us all to be together."

25

EVA

Eva hoped Sam would be waiting for them outside, but she was disappointed. Outside the pyramid, the cold night air had a bite to it. Smoke hung heavily all around but there was no sign of Sam. There was no sign of anyone but the jet and its crew, who had refueled and returned to the landing site.

"What do we do?" Eva asked Lora.

"We wait," she replied.

"No word from them?" Alex asked.

"Communications in Cairo are rather sporadic right now," Phoebe said. "Jedi and Shiva are working on it." She turned to look at them. They were a little way off, fiddling with their equipment. "But Sam and the Professor know that this is the rendezvous, so we wait here."

Dr. Dark came over with Xavier. The rest of the last 13 sat with Phoebe, setting up a small campfire. News of Ahmed and the director had filtered through the group and Xavier had taken the death of his godfather very hard. Eva could see Phoebe was struggling with the loss of the director but was determined to keep the focus on the race to the Dream Gate.

Eva looked up at the stars.

There's not much time left to put together the Bakhu.

Where are you, Sam?

"We're so close," Alex said out loud. "It seems impossible. I mean—it's hard to imagine such an awesome machine being created so long ago. And that when it's put together, it's gonna reveal something of even greater . . . awesomeness?"

Despite herself, Eva chuckled.

"We all must go to the Gate with an open mind," Dr. Dark said, his arm still around Xavier. "It will truly be an important discovery—or rediscovery, as it were. We really won't know what it can do until we open it."

"But, with Solaris as the last Dreamer, *will* we be able to open it?" Eva said. "And how can we—"

"Wait, what did you say?" Phoebe interrupted.

"Oh man," Alex said.

"Sam had his last dream in London," Lora said.

"Are you kidding?" Cody said. "*Solaris* is one of us?"

There was an uneasy silence as those who knew of Sam's dream nodded slowly. They were greeted by grim faces all around. Phoebe pulled Lora aside and began a whispered conversation with her, Dr. Dark joining them.

"But there's still twelve of us and only one of him," Rapha said.

"Yeah, but now there's no way to avoid having him at the Gate with us," Xavier said.

"Not if we want to fulfill the prophecy, correct?" Poh added.

"Look, there's no point getting worked up about it now," Jedi said. "Our first priority is meeting up with Sam and the Professor. Then we can worry about Solaris."

Lora and the others came back, Dr. Dark moving to Xavier's side. "How are you holding up, son?" he asked.

"Pretty good, considering," Xavier joked. "But you can imagine we're all a bit freaked out about what's going to happen at the Gate. We still don't really know what the Dream Gate *does*."

"Maybe it allows people to enter the Dreamscape while awake?" Eva said. "Could that be the power of the Gate?"

"Perhaps, Eva," Dr. Dark said. "But it's crucial to think of the Gate in the context of its creation, back in Ancient Egypt, in the time of Ramses."

"OK," Cody said, "go on . . ."

"Think of it like this—what are the biggest structures we build today?" Dr. Dark said.

"Sports stadiums," Alex said. "Airports?"

"Roads, bridges, tunnels," Eva added, "and skyscrapers."

"They're big, sure, but are they the biggest?" Dr. Dark said, letting the thought linger for a while. "How about hydroelectric dams? The ones that create energy from water moving through turbines."

"I don't get how any of this has anything to do with the Dream Gate," Alex said. "I mean, dams, power, big deal."

"Electrical charges have been registered at the top of the pyramids. And other places have similar properties."

Issey, Arianna and Poh moved closer, listening intently.

"And as we've just seen," Dr. Dark said, "deep under the Giza Plateau," he gave a sweep of his hand, "there are man-made labyrinths of water tunnels that zigzag from the Nile, that combined with the sun's rays and the appropriate pressure could, well, *could* create power."

"Power?" Xavier asked.

"Absolutely," Dr. Dark said. "In only the last few years, scientists discovered a new way of generating electricity using water, the first new method for centuries. Imagine having access to clean, non-polluting power."

"But if they had power back then, why haven't we seen evidence of it?" Alex said. "I mean, I don't think the ancient peoples of the world had electric lights and TVs."

"No, I don't think they did either," Dr. Dark said, "but there's a lot we still don't know about ancient history. Some people believe that the stones used in the pyramids form a battery, a storage device for power. The king's chamber is made of granite, so it could be an 'engine room.' Granite under so much pressure creates its own perpetual energy, just like the quartz crystal in a watch."

"So you're saying the pyramids were some kind of machine, rather than a fancy grave for pharaohs?" Eva said.

"Possibly," Dr. Dark said.

"But machines?" Eva said, looking up at the massive building of stone. "I mean, that's—that's amazing!"

"Amazingly *crazy*," Lora chimed in. "It's a theory, Eva, nothing more. One of *many* theories about what these were built for and what the Dream Gate could possibly lead to."

"What's—is that . . . does anyone . . . ?" Alex said, walking away with a curious look on his face.

"Alex?" Eva asked, watching him. "What is it?"

"Look at that, up there," Alex said, pointing to the top of the pyramid. "There are *people* up there!"

Eva squinted, trying to focus in the darkness. As her eyes settled there, she could make out pinpricks of lights and a handful of tiny figures on top of the Great Pyramid, their silhouettes hard to see against the night.

Lora grabbed a pair of night-vision binoculars. She put them to her eyes, staring at the top of the pyramid.

She pulled them away from her face almost instantly. She turned to the others, her face ashen. "The rest of the last 13 are already here."

SAM

The Bakhu was complete.

Sam, Solaris and the Professor stood back and took it in.

Solaris carefully turned the handle. Sam watched as the Gears spun and whirred. The Professor's eyes were wide in silent awe.

"Yes!" Solaris' pleasure at seeing the machine come to life was almost as tangible as Sam's disappointment that he was not the one to do it. Sam looked up to the evening sky—the moon continued its steady rise and more and more stars were puncturing the heavens above them.

Sam looked down and saw a jet below. It sat there, waiting.

The others must have already gotten here. Where are they?

"We wait, up here," Solaris said, looking around at the sky, "until the stars and moon are in the right alignment."

They sat in silence, waiting. Sam glanced at the Professor. He looked old, all of a sudden. The emotional horror of discovering Sebastian was their enemy was taking its toll. He'd tried to speak to his son but Solaris had brushed off the Professor's words, sitting on the opposite side of the pyramid, waiting, watching the moon rise.

As Sam's mind wandered, going back over the events of the last few months and all the adventures he'd had, he glanced down once more at the jet and was startled to see something had changed. There was a campfire down there now, people gathered around it. He couldn't make them out clearly enough to recognize anyone—were they friends, or enemies?

Sam looked out at the clouds of dark smoke that rose from Cairo.

Solaris stood up abruptly. "Time to find out if this race was truly worth it," he said, pointing up at the sky. "Any moment now . . ."

Sam looked up. The full moon was now almost directly

above them. But that wasn't what Solaris was pointing at. He was pointing at a cluster of stars, a constellation opposite Orion.

Ophiuchus.

Solaris held up the machine. He turned Sam's Gear, the key.

CLICK.

The machine whirred. Solaris held it in both hands. He turned the handle to line up the tiny holes through the Gears with the Ophiuchus constellation in the sky. The Gears cranked and clanged, turning around and spinning until—

CLONK!

It stopped.

Solaris looked at the last Gear, the astrolabe, visible on the top of the machine. It lined up with notches that lined the inside of the box.

"What are these markers?" Sam asked, almost to himself.

Nudging ever closer, it was the Professor who replied. "Each represents a specific distance. According to da Vinci's journal, each is a thousand cubits."

"Cubits?" Sam said.

Solaris snorted. "An Ancient Egyptian measurement—about eighteen inches," he said. "You really don't know what you're doing, do you? Some hero . . ."

Sam could feel the Professor's steadying gaze on him.

Solaris tapped on a small screen on the inside of his wrist. Sam could see that it brought up a map with a blinking marker that was zooming in on a location.

"Yes! It's working!" Sam couldn't contain the thrill of seeing the machine finally work. The marker became fixed, blinking in place now.

"That's it!" Solaris turned to Sam with what almost felt like shared excitement. But the moment passed in an instant and Solaris gave the machine to Sam with a rough shove. "Now, how about we get your friends down there to give us a ride?"

27

GABRIELLA

Gabriella watched as Eva took the binoculars. She was glued to them for a long moment, then turned back to the others.

"They're up there—Sam, the Professor and Solaris. But Solaris has two men with him, I think they've got them captive. The Professor was waving down to us and Sam had the Bakhu machine in his arms."

"Have they put it together, do you think?" Gabriella gasped. "It must be, no?"

"It's a long hike back down from there, especially for the Professor," Lora said.

"What are you suggesting?" Xavier said.

"I think we need to take the jet up there and winch them up," Lora replied.

"Are you *crazy?*" Gabriella cried, several of the others nodding in agreement.

Have they forgotten how much that man wanted to hurt us?

"No, Lora's right," Phoebe said. "We have to. Like it or not—and I don't—we need *all* of the last 13 together to open the Dream Gate."

"So we play along, for now," Lora said. "We take the jet up there, winch them aboard, find out where we have to go. We take care of Solaris and his men whenever and however we can."

"I agree," Dr. Dark said. "There is no other way."

"OK, we're moving, now," Lora said, heading towards the jet. She waved at the pilots to start up the engines. "Everyone on board. And keep your wits about you, this is going to be tricky."

"Let's do this," Alex said.

Questo è matto!

The jet roared straight up into the sky and then tilted towards the top of the pyramid. Gabriella was glued to her window, Maria and Xavier next to her. The others were spread out in the rows behind, Phoebe and Lora closest to the door. She watched as they circled the top of the pyramid, the aircraft's powerful lights bathing it in their harsh glare.

Sam, the Professor and Solaris looked up, shielding their eyes from the dust whipping up as the jet hovered directly above them.

Lora opened the cabin door and tossed out a harness and rope attached to a winch. The sound of the jet's engines was almost deafening with the door open.

Gabriella looked below. The machine had been put into Sam's backpack. He had it strapped on tight as he slung the harness over his head and under his arms. He gave a thumbs-up.

Phoebe threw a switch and the winch whirred into action.

"Sam's coming up," Lora announced into the cabin.

It was hard to be excited when they knew Solaris would soon be joining them. Everyone's faces were a mixture of relief and anxiety.

Sam rose up slowly, spinning above the pyramid, his arms and legs tucked in. Near the jet, he disappeared from view for a moment, but as Gabriella leaned forward anxiously, she saw Phoebe and Lora reach down and help him on board. Everyone cheered and called out to Sam as he stood there smiling, just for a second, before his face clouded over.

It's not finished—it's just started.

"You found it?" Dr. Dark asked eagerly. "The machine worked?"

"Yes," Sam said. He looked at everyone in the cabin, drinking in all their faces, all of them together. "It worked, just like they said it would—the world's first GPS."

"Where does it point to?" Shiva said.

"Solaris has it programmed into a map on his wrist," Sam said. "We need him in any case. He's the last of the 13

. . . we can't open the Gate without him. And we can't leave the Professor."

Gabriella watched as first Dr. Dark, then Phoebe and finally Lora all nodded in agreement.

Lora unhooked Sam from the harness, tossed it out the open door and let the rope wind out.

Solaris' men came up next, expertly keeping a tight hold of their guns as they came on board. They spread out, one sitting close to the winch, the other pushing through the rows of seats to stand at the back of the jet, behind the last 13. He leered at Gabriella and Maria as they turned around to glare at him.

This is not good.

Sam crashed down into a seat next to Eva and Alex, across the aisle from Gabriella, Maria and Xavier. He gently rested his backpack on the cabin floor between them.

"You guys OK?" Sam asked.

"We're fine," Eva said. "But we had a run-in with Stella and her men."

"You should have seen her, Sam," Alex said, pointing to Eva. "She was whomping those guys all over the place."

"And Xavier too," Gabriella added with a smile. "All of us, I think."

"So where's Stella now?" Sam asked. "Please tell me she's knocked out and tied up someplace dark and cold . . ." he trailed off at the sight of their faces. "What?"

"She picked a fight with Lora," Eva said, "and then she fell . . . she's dead, Sam."

"Wow," Sam said, leaning back in the chair. "That's . . . huh. I've got a bit to catch up on."

He doesn't even know about the others yet. Dio mio!

But there was no time to fill Sam in as the Professor came into the cabin, Jedi jumping up to greet him.

The winch sprung to life for the final time.

Solaris hung on to the harness with a strong mechanical grip, coming closer with every passing second. His soldier stepped forward to bring him on board, the other raising his gun to show he had his eye on the others. Lora edged back from the door as Solaris appeared, Phoebe moving to stand in front of her.

As Phoebe shut the cabin door, Solaris pulled himself up to his full height, surveying the group as they tried to hide their fear. Gabriella forced herself not to shrink back from him, but the memory of that terrifying night in Rome came flooding back. Turning to Xavier and Maria, she could see their nightmares flashing before their eyes too. She grabbed their hands and squeezed tight.

We can do it, if we stick together. We must believe it.

The world needs us.

Lora looked as if she was about to jump out of her skin, all jangling nerves and barely restrained anger. Her face flushed a deep red and both Phoebe and Jedi held on to her arms.

Please don't do anything stupid, Lora. We need you.

"I hear your second-in-command is no longer with us," Sam said, squaring up to Solaris. There was no reaction from him. "Didn't you hear me?" Sam went on. "Stella's dead!"

Solaris simply shrugged his shoulders and turned on his heel to go forward to the pilots, barking out coordinates. The jet roared off into a slow turn, heading north.

He doesn't care about anyone, not even his own people.

Solaris stalked back to the main cabin. "So here we all are, at long last. The thirteen of us together. Feels like . . . *destiny*," he mocked.

He turned to Lora, his head tilting to one side. Sam moved towards her, Lora's eyes now filling with tears as she came face-to-face with her boyfriend, the one she thought she'd lost, the one she'd grieved for.

Gabriella felt her own eyes grow wet as she witnessed Lora struggle to control her emotions.

"I—I thought you . . ." Lora began. "How could you let us think . . . what *happened* to you?"

"Enough!" Solaris roared, darting forward to seize the Professor by the neck.

Everyone was on their feet, shouting at once.

"Let him go!"

"You've got what you wanted, leave him alone!"

Gabriella heard Sam mutter, "Your time is nearly up," and saw Eva hold him back.

Solaris waved them all away. "Save your pathetic noises. And mark *my* words—anyone tries anything and *Daddy* here is the first to go."

SAM

After a short, tense ride, during which no one spoke, the jet started to make a descent. Sam looked at his watch.

Barely fifteen minutes in the air. We're still in Egypt.

They touched down in the widest section of a dry riverbed. Jedi and Shiva passed out flashlights to everyone. Solaris was the first to the exit, pushing the Professor out in front of him, his wrist-mounted flame weapon pointed at his father's head. They jumped down one by one, switching on their flashlights to light up the enveloping darkness.

"Keep walking up this riverbed until I say otherwise. We'll be watching you all, and if there's anything I don't like, the Professor will feel my wrath. Got it?"

The group was silent.

"UNDERSTAND?" Solaris screamed.

"Yes!" Sam and the others muttered. "Got it."

The whole group set off after him, guided only by their flashlights and the light of the moon and the stars.

"'Dream a path through time and space,'" Eva said, "'there to find the sacred place.'"

"The final lines of the prophecy," Sam said.

"So 'time and space' is referring to the night sky?" Alex asked.

"Gotta be," Sam replied.

"And 'sacred place' . . . maybe we're looking for a temple? And the Dream Gate is hidden there?"

"But where *are* we?" Sam whispered.

"Near a small village called Qantir," Alex said, reading a crumpled map he'd found in the jet. They stumbled on in the dark, the rest of the last 13 fanned out behind them. Solaris remained out in front, checking the coordinates, his burly mercenaries prodding them on. "It's to the east of the Nile delta, about sixty miles north of Cairo."

"It just kills me that we're walking right to the Dream Gate with *him*," Sam said, motioning at Solaris, "and there's not a thing we can do about it."

"Not now," Alex said, "but we'll get our chance. And we'll have to be ready to take it."

"So why do you think the Bakhu brought us here?" Sam said, changing the subject as Xavier and Zara came up behind them to listen in. Underfoot, the riverbed cracked and crumbled with every step.

"Maybe there is a link to Ramses," Zara volunteered. "This area near the delta is meant to be where he built his palace. But the Nile shifted course and there was no more water so they moved on."

"How do you know *that*?" Xavier said, impressed.

"I read," Zara said. "What do you think I've been doing all these weeks while we've been waiting for Sam to find thirteen of us?"

"Right," Xavier said, "fair enough."

"The Ramses connection would make sense," Eva said. "Maybe the Dream Gate was in the most obvious place all along—right where Ramses lived and ruled."

"Out here?" Alex said. "There's nothing . . ."

"Perhaps it's hidden," Eva said.

"How do you hide a *temple*?" Alex asked.

They walked on, each of them thinking, Sam knew, of what they might find and how they might beat Solaris.

But can we stop Solaris if he manages to open the Gate?

"Wait," Solaris commanded, his metallic voice loud in the still night. "Stop here."

They gathered in a group, the Professor, Lora and the others trying to stand protectively between Solaris and the rest of the last 13. Sam saw Phoebe shiver in the cold air but her expression was determined. They were far enough north of Cairo that the air was clear of smoke. The last gasps of a sea breeze blew in from the Mediterranean Sea to the north.

It's time to save the world but it feels like we're a million miles away from everyone else on the planet.

It all comes down to this handful of people in the middle of nowhere.

Is this what Ramses and da Vinci had in mind?

How shocked would they have been to discover Solaris was part of the last 13?

I guess you can't have good without evil to push against it.

"Stay where you are!" Solaris ordered, pacing ahead and checking the map on his wrist, using it to get to the exact spot that the machine had pointed to. He stopped, hesitating, going over the coordinates again.

"Maybe it's gone," Alex said, "been wiped off the map."

"It can't be," Gabriella said. "Not after everything we've gone through."

The riverbed flattened out to a large space, where several old rivers must have met and joined to pour out into sea.

"This is it," Sam said to them, "it's here. But Eva's right—it's hidden someplace."

"The Dream Gate is *here?*" Xavier said, looking around. "I see dry riverbeds. I see embankments, dusty fields and a few rocks."

"But there's nothing here," Cody countered. "Certainly no city."

"Well, there was until the water diverted," Xavier said. "With no water, the city would have been unlivable and abandoned. Over time, it became ruins and then nothing. Zara was just telling us, right?" he added as Zara grimaced at him.

Sam looked around. There were no ruins in sight now. Nothing but small sand dunes and the tops of the old riverbeds, some towering up to thirteen feet high, topped with tufts of desert grass.

“So,” Alex said. “What do we do now?”

“We wait,” Sam said, sitting down, watching Solaris pacing and checking his GPS. “We wait.”

“No,” Solaris said, marching over and pulling out spades from his men’s packs. He pointed to a mound in the center of the riverbed. The river had forked into three streams, leaving a small island of dry dirt and rock. “You don’t wait—you *dig*.”

29

THE LAST THIRTEEN

Sam took a spade from Rapha to carry on digging, the others handing their spades over to the next shift. The first six now sat at the end of the island, spent from half an hour's backbreaking work. The Professor looked pale as he dug next to him. Lora looked furious. Piles of sand and rubble had been excavated, and they were nearly three feet down across a twenty-foot-diameter hole. Solaris watched over them as though he was running a team of slaves.

Is this how Ramses built his city?

"You see a way out of this yet?" Sam whispered to Lora, next to him.

"Not yet . . ." she said through a heavy breath.

"We could rush them with the shovels," Cody muttered.

"Uh-uh," Lora said. "I don't think so."

"It's too dangerous," Sam whispered. "We'll get a chance. Right, Lora?"

Lora nodded.

"Quiet!" Solaris boomed. "Keep digging!"

They continued to dig, the cool night air giving faint relief as they sweated and strained in the ever-widening hole. At Solaris' command, they swapped once more, fresher hands taking over the digging.

"Hey!" Xavier called out suddenly. "I found something!"

Sam scrambled out to stand next to the Professor, looking down at the excavated site lit by the beams of their flashlights. He had to admit, the sight was underwhelming.

All this effort for that? The Dream Gate is something the size of a large wheel?

"Clean it off!" Solaris commanded. "Clear it, quickly!"

Those in the pit dug and scraped with the shovels until they had uncovered the object down to the stone ground beneath it.

It's definitely man-made and looks like it was a part of something . . . but what?

"That's it?" Xavier said, standing back. "*That's* the Dream Gate?"

"Maybe it turns," Alex said, and he heaved and twisted with all his weight. "Impossible."

"Help him!" Solaris commanded.

Alex, Poh, Cody, Maria, Rapha and Issey crowded around, their hands wrapped around the tube-like shaft that formed a ring. They twisted, trying each way. Nothing—there was no movement at all.

"OK," Issey said. "Maybe this isn't something that turns, but some kind of ornament."

Clean from most of the dirt now, it was clearly a bronze wheel, sitting flat, like a tabletop. It was connected by a metal shaft to a waist-height pedestal, which in turn was on top of a stone platform.

"This looks like a bigger version of the Schist Disk," Alex said, shining his flashlight closer.

"The what?" Eva asked.

"A thing that Ahmed showed me," Alex said, using his hands to brush out as much sand as he could from where the connecting shaft met the stone. "That one's much smaller. It's made from a type of stone called schist. It was found in a dig somewhere in southern Egypt. Weird thing is, it's dated to thousands of years *before* Egypt had the wheel."

"Sam," Solaris said. "Get back down there. Tell me what you see."

Sam didn't say anything, he just slid down the lip of the sand wall they had created and landed with a thud. He went over to the wheel. It was bigger than a car's steering wheel—more like the one on his school bus. He rubbed the surface at the middle and it shone with a dull glow. Sam crouched down. The wheel was attached to a bronze pedestal.

"It seems like it *should* turn," Sam said, standing up. "There are marks on the shaft, as though it spins down."

Sam gripped the rim and twisted. It wouldn't budge for him either.

He tried the other way—nothing.

He pushed and pulled with all his strength and weight. Still nothing.

"All of you," Solaris said. "Get down there and open it!"

As the others began to climb down onto the platform, Lora stepped forward for a better look. "Ah, Sam . . ." she said, looking over his shoulder. She pointed at the top of the wheel with her flashlight.

"What?" Sam said. "I don't see anything."

"Look," she said, using her sleeve to rub the wheel. There was an odd collection of holes in the center of the disk.

The pattern of the holes looked familiar somehow.

I've seen those before, but where?

And then it came to him in a flash. The crank—Zara's Gear had four spikes to it, just like the four holes now in front of them.

Sam climbed back up and knelt down where he'd left his backpack. Opening it up and hefting out the machine, he removed the crank and returned to the wheel below. The crank would not fit—the holes were just a pattern, made with some kind of inlaid blue metal or jewel.

"It's solid," Sam said.

"It's a lid!" Eva said. "Look."

There was a tiny dot of silver at one end and she pushed

against it—a small hinge threw back the lid. Underneath, the same alignment of holes were cut out.

Sam inserted the crank and turned it. It spun around once and then stopped.

CLINK!

"It unlocked the wheel!" Alex said.

"OK, all of us, on three," Sam said, getting into position, the wheel just big enough for all the hands gathered around it.

"One," Eva said.

"Two," Alex said.

"Three!" Sam said.

They moved as one and the wheel grudgingly shuddered and nudged around. As a group they took a step to their right, and then another, keeping their hands wrapped tight around the wheel as they shifted around. When the wheel had spun around once, it stopped dead with a loud bang.

"Is it stuck?" Alex asked.

"No," Sam replied, crouching down and looking under the wheel. It seemed to drop down a tiny bit, as though it was meant to reach that point and then halt. "That was it. That's all it does."

"What's going on?" Solaris called out. "What's happening down there?"

"Why don't you come down and take a look for yourself?" Alex shouted at him.

PFFT!

A dart shot close by Alex's head.

"The next one won't miss, boy," Solaris said. "Now, all of you, keep turning that—"

Solaris stopped talking, because at the moment, a rumbling noise emanated from all around the island. It grew louder and louder.

WHOOSH!

Sam scrambled up the wall of excavated sand to stand next to Solaris and the Professor. He got there in time to see water spouting out from thirteen points around the island. It gushed straight out, horizontally, under enormous pressure. It blasted out onto the dry riverbeds around them where it was instantly soaked up into the dusty ground.

"Professor?" Sam asked. "What do you think . . . ?"

"I'm not sure," the Professor said. "But I think this is just the beginning of something."

"Great," Alex said, now next to Sam. "It's a fountain. Solaris has led us to a long lost—"

Then he fell over. Everyone on the island did, even Solaris, spilling down into the excavated pit. They were rolling around in the large hole, everyone moving, no one still.

But it wasn't just them—the whole *pit* was moving.

Up.

The round area they had excavated rose up into the air, with them on it. Within a second the wheel was level with the ridge of the riverbank, and in another it was seven feet above it, rising rapidly. It was as though they were now standing on top of a tall tower in the middle of a desert.

In the momentary confusion, Lora saw her opportunity and pounced.

She rolled towards Solaris' henchman, Pike, and landed two punches before she was shoved away. But she threw out a leg as she fell, catching him off balance and tipping him off the rising platform. He landed in the rushing water below.

BANG!

Phoebe smacked a heavy shovel into the back of Solaris' head, but he barely registered the impact.

The suit, it's acting like armor!

Solaris spun around, steadying himself on the moving earth and kicked Phoebe clear off the platform and she fell from the edge with a scream.

"Mom!" Alex lunged for her but she was gone. Searching for her, he spotted her waving from the water down below.

"I'm OK," she yelled out. "Fight, Alex, fight!"

Alex stood up and turned on Solaris but he had grabbed the person closest to him—Eva. He held his flame weapon up to her neck as she fought against him. Everyone else moved closer in, circling Solaris and his one remaining guard. But they were thrown here and there as the platform kept rising until it finally stopped with a shudder.

Sam moved slowly to the edge to look down, discovering

that there was another platform underneath them, columns all around—holding up the platform they stood on.

"It *is* a temple," Maria said, looking down. "A temple, hidden in the desert."

"A sacred place . . ." Alex said.

"This is no ordinary temple," Solaris murmured. "This is *it*. This is the Dream Gate."

At that, another noise started up—a harsh, whirring sound.

"Look out!" Poh said, moving back from the wheel, which was now turning, fast. But now it was turning the opposite way from before.

As they watched, the thirteen water spouts died down to a steady cascade, and the center of their platform, with the bronze wheel on top, started to twist upward, further into the sky, fifteen, thirty, sixty feet tall, at least, until it stopped with a mechanical clank. It now looked like a tall antenna.

"There are stairs in here . . ." Xavier said, walking around the tall bronze tower. "They don't lead up, but they go down—we can get to the level below."

"Do it!" Solaris said, keeping a tight grip on Eva. "Anyone tries to get clever, I roast you, one by one, starting with her. And then I'll drag your carcasses down there. I'm not sure the prophecy needs all of the last 13 to be *alive*." He signaled to his remaining man. "Holt, make sure all the children behave themselves, won't you?"

Holt nodded and began pushing everyone towards the stairs. Eva started down first, desperately trying to catch Sam's eye, Solaris close behind her. The others followed, the Professor and Sam last. The stairs were tiny and wrapped in a tight spiral.

By the lights of their flashlights, they could see ornate statues in between the columns and some large rectangular stones set around the edges of the chamber. Sam caught a glimpse of Roman numerals carved into the floor in front of each stone. What was odd was that it seemed as though his flashlight shone *into* the floor, like it was made out of some kind of black glass.

Crystal. The same kind that surrounded the Star of Egypt.

"Get onto your numbers," Solaris said, sweeping his light around and picking out the numbers.

"What?" Alex said.

"Your order in the last 13," Sam said, the realization hitting him also, "so Solaris is one, Alex two, Eva three, all the way back to me." The numbers were fanned out like the face of a clock.

They moved around each other, searching out their numbers—Gabriella found twelve quickly, Arianna opposite her, Eva on the other side from Rapha. The others slotted between them, standing in front of each slab, made from the same crystal.

"But what about you?" Alex said to Sam, looking twitchy next to Solaris.

"I know where I have to stand," Sam said, shining his flashlight to the middle of the platform, next to the staircase. There was the number that had been haunting him for so long now—XIII.

Feeling everyone's eyes on him, Sam slowly walked towards the center. He looked around at his friends. They all looked scared, apprehensive. He felt sick.

Here goes nothing . . . or everything.

He stepped gently onto the carved numeral—and waited.

At first, there was nothing. Only the sound of anxious breathing in the chill night air. Flashlight beams flitted around the circle as they looked at each other, afraid, excited, curious.

And then . . . their world lit up. Not around them but *under* them.

The whole crystal disk under their feet started to glow. It was dull at first, then brighter and brighter, until a light flashed as bright as the sun. Sam reeled back and shielded his eyes.

The last 13 was complete.

Sam jumped aside as the ground beneath his feet shifted. The Roman numeral was twisting and turning, a small disk in the floor rising up until it was almost level with his waist. Squinting in the light from the floor, Sam looked closer. Right there within the XIII, a star-shaped hole was now visible. The ultimate keyhole for Sam's key.

This is it, this is how you open the Dream Gate!

Sam looked at the key in his hand, reaching over to insert it.

"Stop!"

Sam spun around. Solaris had Alex by the throat, his weapon pointed at him. "Give me the key and your friends live." Holt had his gun aimed at Eva. Sam could see Jedi flinching out of the corner of his eye.

"Don't do it, Sam!" Eva yelled out.

"You can't let him open the Gate . . ." Alex began, faltering as Solaris smacked his armored fist into the side of Alex's head.

Sam hesitated, the conflict within him clearly etched on his face. He turned to glance at the Professor and Lora but he couldn't read their faces. Jedi and Shiva looked on helplessly.

What do I do?

Unbidden, memories of Bill flashed through Sam's mind. A friend lost, someone he couldn't save.

But I can save them.

Sam came forward with his arm outstretched, the key dangling from its strap. Solaris reached over and snatched it from him, shoving Alex to the floor.

In three quick strides, Solaris was at the pedestal, his black mask taking on even greater menace in the glow from the floor.

"No!"

"Don't do it!"

"Wait!"

But Solaris wasn't listening. He forced the key into the lock, turning it with a triumphant flourish.

Everyone fell to the floor, screaming.

31

"Make it stop!"

"Help me!"

"Argh!"

"No, *please!*"

The fire was everywhere, overwhelming Sam as the cries of the others mingled with his own and the cries of millions all over the world.

The heat, the frightening flames, the loss of Bill, Solaris chasing him at every turn, fire always a heartbeat away—the memories and images came crashing over him. His worst nightmare repeating over and over before his eyes.

My worst nightmare.

I have to stop it, stop the nightmares for everyone.

Sam forced his eyes open and took in the shocking scene. Everyone was crying out, doubled over, plagued by their own personal nightmares—the dark, heights, being alone, drowning—everyone trapped in a mental prison of their worst fears.

Sam forced himself to see past the images of Bill,

standing up slowly as he saw Lora lurching in terror and Cody grabbing hold of Maria, each trying to steady the other. Sam spun around, seeing them all panicked—Rapha, Eva and Alex huddled together, Gabriella and Zara, Arianna, Xavier and Poh, Issey—all trying to beat back the horror, to regain control. Even the Professor was fighting to stay in the moment, pushing against the fears in his nightmares.

Sam turned finally to face Solaris, the cold mask betraying nothing within.

Does he not feel it?

"What have you done?" Sam gasped. He glimpsed the horizon in the distance. It looked as though it was on fire, a wall of red. As Sam struggled to stay upright, he saw the sky turn the red-orange of the sun, spreading out through the atmosphere.

Sam began to move towards Solaris, nothing but sheer force of will propelling him forward as he swung high to take Solaris down.

He crashed into Solaris, seeming to have the upper hand for a moment. They landed heavily, skidding across the crystal floor to slam into a statue that lurched dangerously above them. Sam pulled away quickly, the falling statue missing him and Solaris by a hair's breadth.

"It's too late," Solaris growled, spinning to his feet. "This won't help you now," he taunted, swinging the key in front of Sam. Sam bolted to grab it but Solaris pulled it away, viciously kicking Sam in the leg, making him double over in agony.

"This is madness!" Sam gasped, clutching at one of the standing stones to haul himself upright.

"Welcome to the new world," Solaris said, grabbing Sam by the neck and slamming him into the crystal stone.

Sam felt his back scream in pain as the stone cracked, shearing off to smash onto the floor, which was now glowing fiery red.

Solaris stepped back, pulling back his arm as his flame weapon clicked into life. He pointed it at Sam, but Sam was already moving—*towards* Solaris. Sam threw himself onto his enemy, grabbing his shoulders and bringing up his knee to slam it into his stomach as he spun him around. Taken by surprise, Solaris stumbled back, flailing as he tripped over the crumbled crystal. Sam grasped hold of Solaris' suit and pushed him away with a mighty heave.

Solaris fell back and then stopped.

The cracked stone had left a broken edge, razor sharp—and deadly.

Solaris let out a bloodcurdling scream as he slid down the crystal, the point piercing his body armor as he fell backward. He hung there for a terrible moment before the shard broke off in his body, letting him fall to the floor in agony.

Through the images of his nightmares, Sam saw that his enemy—the *world's* enemy—was fatally injured.

He'd finally done it.

Sam had defeated Solaris.

"Give me the key!" Sam said, leaning over Solaris, pulling away the tubes in his suit so the flames could not hurt him anymore. Solaris' moans filled the air.

"Get away from him, Sam!"

Sam spun around, searching the faces swimming before him through his nightmare haze.

Who said that? Solaris' guard, Holt?

But Holt was lying prone on the ground—someone had taken care of him while Sam had taken on Solaris.

Then who?

From among the last 13, who all stumbled forward, another pushed to the front.

"I said, get away from him!"

Dr. Dark stood before Sam, a gun pointed at Sam's head.

What?

"Are you kidding?" Sam stammered. "What are you doing? I need the key. Maybe we can still fix what Solaris has done."

"I know," Dr. Dark said, still moving forward, now nudging Sam away with his gun, standing next to Solaris as he lay bleeding on the floor. He reached down and pulled the key from Solaris' grasp. "He has done well, but alas I think his time has come. Mine, however, is just beginning."

"Dark?" The Professor came forward, leaning on Eva as everyone tried to fight through their fears to comprehend what was happening.

"Spare me the high ground, Professor," Dr. Dark said. "I don't need to listen to your moralizing lectures anymore. Just stand there and accept that you've lost. All this time you were all concentrating so hard on beating Solaris, you never stopped to consider who the real enemy was."

"*Dad?*" It was Xavier, coming closer with Arianna, his face ashen with fear, but now with something else. "What are you—how can you be . . . ?" He was at a loss for words in the face of such inconceivable betrayal.

"Xavier . . . perhaps my one regret was you. I didn't know you'd end up being one of the 13. That was a complete surprise." His face clouded for a moment. "So you see, I never thought you'd be here at the end, at the Gate."

"Are you saying you're on *his* side? That you have been all along?" Xavier stammered.

"More like he's been on *my* side," Dr. Dark smirked. "A useful puppet to be sure, vicious and unrelenting." He turned to look at Solaris. "I am sorry that you won't live to see our vision realized."

Solaris gasped, pulling at the mask. The Professor came forward, ignoring Dr. Dark and his gun as he knelt down next to Solaris. Carefully, he pulled off the mask, everyone gasping audibly at the shock of seeing Sebastian's face once more. Jedi made to come forward too, but checked himself. Lora could only look away as he lay dying.

"Don't give me your pity," Sebastian said, "don't you *dare*." His eyes narrowed, glancing around them. "You deserve what's coming, all of you. Now you'll know what it's like to have your worst nightmare come true, to live without hope and feel lost—forever."

"How can you say that?" the Professor said, shocked. "I know losing your mother changed you, made you hate the world. But this is not the way. You cannot answer darkness by pulling others into it, you have to step out into the light."

"But I didn't want to," Sebastian muttered. "I *liked* the darkness." His body was racked with spasms as he fell from the Professor's arms and slumped to the ground.

Sebastian—Solaris—was dead.

In the stunned silence, all eyes turned to Dr. Dark, who clutched his gun tighter. The key swung from his grip, tantalizingly close.

"I don't understand," Xavier said, moving towards his father as he circled around them all. "Everything you've ever taught me, that you've believed in and stood for. My whole life—it's been a *lie*? All your work, research . . . and Ahmed? He *died* trying to get here, trying to help us!"

"There's no need to be melodramatic," Dr. Dark said. "Children never really know their parents. Consider this a rare insight. And don't lose any sleep over Kader, he was in it up to his neck. He worked for *me*, he knew exactly what I was planning and it's all just—"

"Shut up!" Xavier screamed. "Don't talk like it doesn't matter. This is the whole world you're talking about! Look around you!" He gestured wildly to the others, all struggling to ignore the terrors of their nightmares.

Sam edged nearer, hoping Dr. Dark's attention on Xavier would give him enough of a moment to attack. But Dr. Dark was hyperalert, swinging around to keep everyone in sight.

How do we get that key?

As if reading his mind, Xavier walked purposefully towards his father, one hand outstretched. "Give me the key."

"Stay back, Xavier," Dr. Dark said, "don't think I won't do it."

"Give me the key," Xavier said again.

"Get back!"

"*No!*" Xavier reached for the key.

A single shot rang out.

Dr. Dark's warning shot skimmed the edge of the roof and ricocheted into the night, Xavier skidding to his side, disbelief on his face. But the distraction was all Sam needed. He snatched the key from Dr. Dark's grasp, turning to run to the center of the floor, his eyes focused only on the pedestal.

"I'll shoot you, Sam!" Dr. Dark roared, firing another shot into the night as he came after him. "Just remember, you don't know me *at all*."

The threat stopped Sam cold, just an arm's length from the pedestal. He turned to face Dr. Dark, seeing Jedi and Lora edging closer to him, Shiva joining them.

Would he really kill me?

Do I have any choice but to take that chance?

"I have to do it," Sam said slowly. "If it's my destiny to die for the world, then so be it." He took another step, his eyes still on Dr. Dark.

"Give me back that key," Dr. Dark said, his voice now low and vicious. "Or I'll kill everyone here, believe me."

"Then you start with me," Eva said, stepping in front of Sam.

"And me," Alex said, joining her.

"Please, no," Sam said, urging them to move aside. "It just has to be me, don't do this."

"We're in this together," Eva said, her teeth gritted as she took Alex's hand. Rapha and Zara were moving towards them, Maria, Poh and Issey stepping forward to block Dr. Dark's path to Sam.

"You're all willing to *die* for him?" Dr. Dark was incredulous. "Don't be *stupid*."

Cody and Gabriella stood firm with them, holding each other's arms and forcing themselves not to flinch from Dr. Dark's gun.

"GIVE ME THAT KEY!" Dr. Dark screamed, veins popping out on his forehead as his rage consumed him.

Xavier came in front of them all. "You'll have to start with *me*," he said.

"Have it your way."

Xavier closed his eyes as his father pulled the trigger, but it was Arianna who took the bullet, pushing Xavier out of the way. "No!" she cried as she slumped to the ground.

"Arianna!"

And in that moment, time seemed to speed up in front of Sam's eyes. Lora was sprinting, jackknifing into Dr. Dark as another shot rang out, the two of them crashing to the ground. But Dr. Dark was up from under her immediately, kicking her viciously as Cody slammed into him with a war cry, Eva on top of them. There was a flurry of arms and legs as others piled into the fight, finally using their numbers to overwhelm him.

Sam saw the gun skid across the floor, the Professor stooping to pick it up, throwing it into the now raging waters below.

And then there was Arianna. She lay on the floor, blood blooming over her chest like a deadly crimson flower. Maria and Issey held her tenderly. Sam rushed over, kneeling to take her hand in his. But it was already cold. Her eyes were closed, her body still.

"She's gone," Issey said, tears in his eyes.

I don't believe it.

Sam's mind refused to grasp the idea that someone so strong, so full of life and fight, could no longer be alive.

She was here just a moment ago . . .

"Sam," Issey said, grasping Sam's arm, "you finish this now, you do it for *her*, you do it for us *all*."

Sam turned to see that the others had wrestled Dr. Dark upright, pinning his arms back as he struggled against them.

"Look what you did," Dr. Dark spat out. "You let that girl die for you. You *coward*."

"*DARK!*" Sam launched himself at his tormentor, ripping him from everyone's grasp, grappling with him as they slid across the crystal floor. Sam attacked him again and again, the strain of all the days of running, fighting, fearing for his life, for the lives of others—the weight of the prophecy, the burden of knowing he was the one who must save the world—pouring out of him in one terrible moment.

"Sam!" Rapha and Alex were pulling him off Dr. Dark. "Sam, *stop!*"

A grinding noise echoed in the air, vibrating through the floor itself. Sam hesitated, even as he still had Dr. Dark in his grasp, his knees holding him down.

Dr. Dark pulled his bloodied face closer to Sam, sneering. He nodded towards the pedestal. "Time's up, Sam," he laughed. "You lose."

Sam turned to see that the pedestal was turning back the other way, going back into the floor.

No!

Sam pulled away, desperate to use the key before it was too late.

But Dr. Dark had one last trick to play. Grabbing Sam squarely with both hands, he rolled them both over the edge of the platform, plunging them towards the violent waters below.

34

"Hold on!"

Xavier clung to Sam's wrists as he dangled over the edge of the platform. Dr. Dark was just below Sam, his hands grasping at the tower's wall, his feet finding purchase on a tiny ledge.

"I've got you, Sam," Xavier called out.

Sam could see Alex and Lora's hands reaching out to help him, pulling him slowly upward as his arms tensed in agony.

I have to make it . . . the key . . .

Sam could see the red glow from the crystal floor above casting an eerie light behind his friends as they looked down at him. The fire dancing before his eyes was so intense, he almost couldn't see. His mind was screaming as much as his arms were and he knew the world was on a nightmare path that only he could stop.

With superhuman effort, Sam pushed himself upward into their waiting arms, their faces speaking of the terrible unseen pain behind their eyes. He flung his arm over the edge onto the floor, Alex grabbing him by the waist and pulling him over until he lay flat on his back, panting for breath.

Sam looked up at anguished faces. "Thanks," he whispered. He turned his head to see that Xavier was crouched over the edge, reaching for his father. Sam scrambled to his feet, the others gathered around Xavier.

Xavier had his arm stretched out to his father as Shiva and Cody held on to him for counterbalance. "Please, Dad, it's never too late. Take my hand."

Dr. Dark's bloodstained grimace made him almost unrecognizable. "It *is* too late, son. For me, you, for everyone. You should step up, take your place in my stead. Rule the world. Don't leave it to weaklings like Sam."

"But, that isn't even . . . I don't understand why you did this," Xavier said.

"You're stronger than you think," he said. "You're a Dark, just like me, don't forget that."

"I'm *nothing* like you," Xavier said defiantly, even as reluctant tears streamed down his face.

The scowl on Dr. Dark's face finally dissolved, replaced by a strange expression.

Fear, maybe . . . not regret.

"Good-bye, Xavier," Dr. Dark said. He let go, plunging down without even a scream, to disappear in the restless torrents beneath them.

Xavier gasped and turned away. Zara rushed forward to embrace him.

"Sam," Jedi said, grasping his arm. "We're out of time."

"I know," Sam said. He forced himself to turn away from his friend's grief, sprinting to the pedestal which had almost sunk back into the glowering floor. The stonework itself was crumbling, falling apart.

It's self-destructing. You open the Gate and that's it.

One chance only.

But I've still got the key.

With shaking hands, Sam grasped the key, holding it up to use it one last time. With his nerves jangling, he slotted it carefully into the pedestal, the dust dancing on top as it shook in the ground. He waited for what seemed like an eternity.

He took a deep breath and closed his eyes, confronting the flames and Bill's face.

Please let this work. Please let this be enough.

And for the smallest, sharpest moment there was silence. Impossible, heavenly silence. Sam could hear no screams, no pounding of the rising water around them, no wind, no heartbeat, no breathing. Just stillness.

Then things changed. The world began to spin again. Thunder seemed to rumble from everywhere at once—an almighty shaking of the sky to break the deathly silence. The floor was changing from fiery red to startling white.

And light shot up all around them.

Sam's eyelids fluttered wildly as he flinched in the overwhelming white, blinding brightness. And then it was gone. He opened his eyes. He was on his knees, collapsed at the pedestal which had now sunk back into the floor, the keyhole disintegrated, the key lying broken next to him.

He glanced around. The last 13, those who remained, stood like statues around him—Jedi, Shiva, the Professor and Lora the same.

Did I do it?

He turned to see Eva's face as she broke out into a smile. "The nightmares, Sam," she said, "they're gone."

That's right!

Bill had left him, the flames had died, he could see clearly now.

Slowly the others came back to life, shaking their heads, cautiously smiling as they came forward.

"You did it!" Gabriella and Alex said as one, as they, Eva and the last 13 crowded around him.

"The Dream Gate belongs to the light," the Professor said warmly as he stepped forward to clasp Sam's hand.

Sam felt his knees shake as the full realization hit him.

It's over.

"Look!" Cody shouted, turning to the south. "What's that?"

Far off in the distance, great blasts of blue light shot into the sky like fireworks, streaking upward and fanning out across the darkness.

"It's the pyramids in Cairo!" Lora said.

A blue-white bolt of electricity arced through the sky.

The shimmering charge split and twisted into millions of tiny flashes. Twin streams of plasma began to circle the tops of the pyramids. They moved like flames chasing a fast wind, snaking their way upward, lasting no more than a minute before vanishing in a final, blinding flash. The double helix pulse was gone as quickly as it had appeared. It pulsed in Sam's eyes for a moment, the negative image burning onto his retinas.

I don't know what that means yet.

But I know it's a good sign.

Sam smiled, but his smile faded as he glimpsed Xavier slumped against a column. Pushing past the others, he knelt down next to him. "There's nothing I can say," Sam began, "but know that we are in this together. You won't be alone—ever."

Xavier turned his face to Sam's, forcing himself to look resolute. "I know. I'm so sorry, Sam. That it was *my* father all along . . . how can I ever . . . ?"

"You are *not* your father's son," Sam said. "You're one of the last 13."

The Professor gathered them together. "You have made me so proud," he said, "and at a time when I thought I would never feel that again. You have saved us all from the nightmare that Sebastian and Dr. Dark wished upon us." He looked directly at Xavier. "But we have prevailed, and that is all that matters in the end. And we will not forget the sacrifices made here today."

As one, they turned to look at Arianna.

We can't ever forget.

"Professor!" Lora said, jolting everyone from their sad thoughts. "I think we have one more problem to worry about." She and Jedi stood at the platform's edge, peering downward. "The water's still rising."

Sam rushed to the edge to look. The churning waters released by the Dream Gate were now almost level with the platform.

The water's going to submerge the Gate! It's meant to reclaim it forever.

What are we going to do?

We cannot have come this far to fail now.

"We must jump in, yes?" Zara said. "Everyone can swim?"

"But . . . what about Arianna, and . . . ?" Xavier looked at the Professor.

"We may have to let the water take them," the Professor said. "I will not let you all perish here. There has been enough death."

Sam came face-to-face with the harsh reality of their situation. As they began to strip off outer layers to plunge into the freezing waters, Eva called out, "Wait! I think there's another way!"

"What? How?" Alex stopped in the middle of pulling off his sweater.

Eva was standing next to the pedestal, where Sam had inserted the key. But now that the pedestal had fallen away, a widening hole revealed a tunnel down through the middle of the tower.

Lora held out a hand. "Hold on, I'll go first," she said. "Shine your flashlights down and I'll see if it really leads somewhere. We don't want to end up trapped under here."

She slipped into the hole, scraping painfully down the rocky edges as she braced against the rim. "Hold on!" she said, training her flashlight directly beneath her. "I can see ledges all the way down! You're right, Eva, this is a way out."

"OK, everyone get ready," Sam said. "We'll go single file after Lora. Professor, you're next."

"I will carry Arianna," Xavier said. "We're not leaving her here." Sam nodded, the tears in Xavier's eyes mirrored in those around him.

"And I will take Sebastian," Rapha said. "He is the Professor's son." Jedi nodded, coming over to help him.

"Thank you," the Professor said quietly, patting Rapha's arm.

"Let's go!" Alex called out from the edge of the descending stairwell. "Lora's already halfway down. It looks good."

One by one, Sam refusing to leave until the last of them had climbed down, they navigated the rough ledges that allowed them to slither and slide down the tunnel. Waiting until everyone was safely inside, Sam stooped to pick up the two pieces of the broken key, gazing at them for a moment before putting them into his pocket. He climbed in after Poh, dragging a large chunk of broken crystal on top of the hole, almost completely blocking it.

Hopefully that'll hold the water back long enough for us to get clear down there.

I hope this is what Ramses had in mind. I hope this is meant to be the escape route.

Sam coughed loudly in the dusty confines of the tunnel. He had to brace with every step, slipping from ledge to ledge, careful not to drop too fast to give Poh enough time ahead of him. As he scrambled down, scraping hands, arms, knees as he dropped, suddenly he felt water splashing onto him.

"Go! Poh, quickly!" Sam urged. His flashlight beam caught his face as he looked up and felt the water beginning to cascade around them.

"The water!" Poh climbed down even faster, urging on the others below him.

Sam could feel his clothes getting soaked as more and more water rained down on him, drenching him and making it harder to keep a grip on the rocky walls.

We're out of time . . . we're going to drown!

Sam felt hopelessness wash over him.

Focus, Sam. Don't give up. Tobias wouldn't give up.

With renewed energy, he forced himself to cling to the now muddy walls, concentrating on not falling onto those below him.

A few seconds later, strong hands reached out to him, pulling him close to the wall and into a side tunnel.

"We've got you!"

Sam sprawled onto the floor, Eva and Alex still holding on to him. Water gushed past them as they huddled together, watching the water fall further down the main tunnel.

"Looks like there's an underground reservoir," Lora said, wrapping her jacket around Sam's shivering shoulders. "In any case, the water isn't going to be following us along here. Come on, Gabriella and Cody are scouting ahead with the Professor and Jedi."

It turned out that they didn't have far to go. They caught up with the Professor and the others in a few minutes. The path underfoot changed from rough-hewn rock to a smoother path, finally turning into paving stones. As they wound around a long bend, they came abruptly to a set of large doors fixed squarely across the tunnel.

"Are these made from copper?" Eva asked, stepping forward to touch the heavy doors, casting her flashlight beam across them, the reflected light bouncing around the dark tunnel.

"Where are we?" Alex said.

"Somewhere no one has been for over three thousand years," Sam said. "These doors are made of *gold*," he said, running his hand over them. "They've been shut all this time, waiting for us."

Everyone stared at Sam as he turned to face them, pointing at a hole halfway down one of the doors.

A hole in the shape of a star.

Sam carefully pulled out the broken pieces of the key, holding the stem in one hand as he slipped the blade of the key into the lock.

Everyone held their breath as Sam delicately nudged it around with the remaining jagged piece of stem, just barely sticking out from the lock.

CLICK.

With that tiny, gentle sound, the door swung open.

"Sam, I think you should do the honors," the Professor said, encouraging him forward.

"OK, time to see what Ramses left us," Sam said quietly. He grabbed both doors and heaved them wide open, stepping across the threshold and across millennia.

A steep staircase of wide steps greeted Sam and he walked down slowly, picking out his way with his flashlight. The air was cold and stale and he shivered as he reached the bottom. He swept the light here and there, quickly realizing this was an enormous cavern as the flashlight beam was swallowed up. In the far corners, objects sparkled and glittered invitingly.

As Sam moved farther in, the others spreading out behind him, he heard their cries of wonder, calling out what they found—gold and jewels and objects dating back to the Ancient Egyptians and even further.

"This is unlike anything we have ever seen and on such a scale," the Professor said, joining Sam at the front. "These artifacts are from the time of Ramses."

"Check this out!" Alex called over, pointing to a crystal sarcophagus, inlaid with sapphires and diamonds, sparkling in the light of his flashlight.

"The pharaohs *didn't* bury their treasure in the pyramids," Eva added. "It's all *here!*"

And there was more to come. At the far end of the cavernous hall was another set of doors. This time, there was no lock.

"Professor?" Sam said, gesturing before him.

They fell silent as the Professor carefully turned an ancient iron handle to push open the ornate doors now in front of them.

The Professor walked in to find a vast stone gallery. "Scrolls," he said, moving down the main aisle, discovering high shelves covered almost every part of the enormous chamber, "thousands of scrolls and carved tablets. And look here—a stele . . . this is a *library!*"

"Like the one that was lost at Alexandria, in the famous fire?" Eva asked, marveling at the rows and rows of scrolls.

"Yes," the Professor replied, "but still here, intact, safe and waiting all these years. Imagine what knowledge, what secrets they must contain!"

"All the secrets lost from ancient civilizations?" Alex said. "Hans was right, and Ahmed."

"Even Dr. Dark talked about technology that had disappeared through history," Maria added. "Sorry, Xavier," she said hurriedly, turning to look at him, apologetic for having brought up Xavier's father.

"It's OK," Xavier said. "I can't pretend he didn't exist. I don't think I even want to, if that doesn't sound crazy."

"It doesn't," Zara said, taking his arm.

"To think, all this was just sitting underground, all these centuries," Sam said, "put here by Ramses, by Dreamers, to protect it, for us." He sighed, sitting down among the rows of shelves, stacked with ancient knowledge, stretching away into darkness, farther than their lights could illuminate.

He was suddenly weary.

The world is saved. And I've saved who I can.

We've found the treasure.

I'm done.

"Me too," Eva said, anticipating his thoughts as she sat down next to him, her arm over his shoulders. The others gravitated towards them—tired, spent, wanting the comfort of each other. Jedi hugged Lora as Shiva grinned and turned to the Professor.

"It has been an incredible journey," the Professor said, "an incredible race. And now we're here with all this knowledge. Lost, and now found. Like us."

He turned to the last 13, smiling at them. "Finding the Dream Gate is not the end, my friends. It is only just the beginning."

37

EPILOGUE

"I'm joined today by the world's most famous Dreamer, probably it's most famous *person* right now," Nora said, "none other than Sam Williams, the leader of the last 13. Thanks for speaking with us today, Sam."

"You're welcome, Nora." Sam smiled, looking at the reporter on the small monitor propped up next to the camera in front of him. "I promised you when our paths crossed in Antarctica that you'd get the world exclusive interview. I'm just pleased we're all still here to do it."

"Well, of course, our audience may not realize that we've previously met," Nora cooed, "and my cameraman Clive and I were only too happy to play a very small part in your race for the Dream Gate. So tell us, can you explain how the amazing 'free power' phenomenon that has transformed the world came about?"

"I wish I could explain it properly," Sam began. "I might need to leave the mechanics of it to the science expert I know you're talking to after me, but for my part, all I know is that the prophecy led us to the Bakhu—"

"That's da Vinci's machine that you had to put together,

the thirteen of you dreaming of a piece of the machine each," Nora chipped in.

"That's right," Sam continued. "We needed to put together the machine so we could uncover the location of the Dream Gate."

"Which turned out to be just north of Cairo," Nora carried on, "close to where historians believed Ramses the Great, the creator of the Dream Gate and the prophecy, had his palace and ruled over Ancient Egypt."

"Exactly," Sam said.

"Although it must have been an unimaginable shock to discover that Solaris, the agent of so much death and destruction during the race, was none other than Sebastian McPherson, the son of the beloved headmaster of the Dreamer Academy . . ."

As a photograph of Sebastian flashed onto the monitor next to Nora's face as she spoke, Sam tuned out, memories rushing in like the waters swirling around the Dream Gate that fateful night.

"Sam?" Nora asked gently. "Are you still with us? I was just saying how doubly shocking it was that the real mastermind was Dr. Xavier Dark, the preeminent psychiatrist and philanthropist. With his son, Xavier, being another of the last 13, that must have been very—"

"Yes, Nora," Sam said, cutting her off. "I'm sure you can appreciate what a sensitive subject that is." He smiled, his eyes trying to communicate to her through the lens of the camera.

Xavier's been through enough. Move on.

"Ahem, quite, well said," Nora said apologetically. "I imagine it must be hard to think back on those events, I know you lost several people close to you during the race." She waited, giving Sam time to compose his thoughts.

We won the race, we did the right thing, did our best.

But there was a price to be paid.

"I'm sorry," Sam said, looking directly at the camera once more, "it's still a fresh wound in many ways. One of the last 13 bravely gave her life so that I could fulfill the prophecy for the good of humanity."

"That would be your Russian friend, Arianna," Nora said. "But her sacrifice made the ultimate difference—you were able to reverse the terrible effects of the Dream Gate being opened by Solaris. There isn't a single person who won't remember those long terrifying minutes when we were assaulted by our worst nightmares. *And* the chaos that erupted around the world as power cut out everywhere, with devastating results."

Sam nodded, a sad smile flickering across his face. "Arianna, and others—Jack Palmer, the head of the Enterprise, countless Guardians and Agents, my friend and teacher Tobias Cole . . ."

"Ah, yes," the reporter said, her voice low. "Tobias Cole, the science teacher from your high school, tragically killed in hostilities in Cambodia."

Sam paused. "Tobias was a great man—a great scientist, and he would have loved what the Dream Gate has provided for us."

"That's right," Nora replied. "When the nightmares stopped, everything had changed. Suddenly there is power in the air, all our electrical appliances are working purely from the energy around us. Lights, phones, even our TV camera and sound equipment there with you."

"Einstein was a Dreamer, you know," Sam said, "and Tesla. Many of our greatest scientists theorized about tapping into the energy within the planet. They would have been amazed to see it at work in the world today. Turns out the technology was there all along, left behind for us by the Ancient Egyptians. It took the last 13 prophecy and the Dream Gate to unleash its potential."

"And the effects of that will be unimaginably huge," Nora enthused. "No more need to mine the planet for fossil fuels, no more harmful emissions. It's certainly a massive victory for the environment and something that's given access to knowledge, information and resources to people who'd otherwise never have them."

"In many ways, it's a rebirth for us as humans," Sam said. "Ramses hid the Gate, the power, all that knowledge, waiting for the prophecy to be fulfilled when we were ready for it. That time is now, we need to act on that, use it as a springboard to do better, *be* better. Look after this beautiful planet, and each other." He stopped, embarrassed. "I didn't mean to preach," he laughed nervously. "But you take my point."

"I do, Sam, I really do," Nora smiled. "It's a great message and one that I hope everyone watching is hearing loud and clear. And if I could ask you one more question?"

"Yes?"

"We know that Gabriella has returned to Italy and is planning to resume her very successful singing career. Likewise, Issey has announced he will be competing in the upcoming international gaming contest in India. But what of the other remaining members of the last 13? What does the future hold for them?"

"Well, Rapha is intending to go back to Brazil. I think he misses the trees." Sam laughed. "And Maria has already gone back to Cuba. She was reunited with her father while the race was happening and wants to spend time with him for now."

"And the others? What of your closest friends, Alex and Eva?"

"They're here with me, along with Xavier, Zara, Poh and Cody. We've got a lot more to learn about being Dreamers, so for now, school's in session."

"Ha! You save the world, but you still have to go to school, just like any other teenager." Nora smiled. "Well, you're an extraordinary young man and I just want to thank you again for taking the time to tell us a little bit about the amazing journey you've had," she said, wrapping up. "I'm sure this is just the first of many interviews you'll be asked to give and I'm sure you'll be very much in demand."

Sam gave a final wave as Nora signed off, and pulled the earpiece out. He stepped down from the high stool he had been perched on in front of the camera and the lights set up in the room.

"Thanks, guys," he said to the film crew, Clive coming around from the camera to shake his hand.

"Nora was sorry she wasn't able to travel here to meet you in person again," Clive said. "Thanks for keeping your word about the interview, man. Good luck, eh?"

Sam shook Clive's hand and slipped out of the room.

The corridor was full of students as Sam mingled in among them. Many called out greetings to him.

"Hey, Sam!"

"How's it going?"

"Love your work, dude!"

Alex and Eva pounced from around a corner. They'd been waiting for him to finish the interview.

"How'd it go?" Alex asked. "Bored with being famous yet?"

"I think I was bored with it before," Sam replied. "You can have it, Alex."

"Cool, thanks!" Alex thumped his shoulder. "Now if you could just put in a good word for me, maybe I'll be on the front page with you next time. At least I made page four." He laughed, showing Sam a page torn out from a newspaper.

4 THE DAILY GLOBE

LAST THIRTEEN
WHERE ARE THEY NOW?

In the weeks that have followed the incredible events in December, when the last 13 Dreamers opened Ramses II's 'Dream Gate', the whole world has been watching and waiting to marvel at the treasures discovered in the hidden catacombs beneath the sand in Egypt. But the real question on everyone's lips is, just who are these extraordinary teenagers who quite literally saved the world from the brink of evil?

We first met Sam Wil-

Eva Kennedy

Alex Robertson

Poh Keo

"Eurgh, why'd they have to use *that* photo of me?" Eva complained.

"Hey, don't worry, everyone would have been looking at me," Alex teased.

"Yeah, whatever. But where's your mom, anyway?" Eva said as they came out into the courtyard, pulling on their winter coats in the frosty alpine air. "I thought she was meeting us here today."

"She's on her way with Shiva," Alex said. "Apparently, now that she's head of the Enterprise, she has lots of very important meetings to go to. Rather her than me!" he said. "But at least with the Enterprise and Academy working together now, I don't have to pick a side." He made a face at Eva.

"Well, I'm just glad they've managed to fix up so much of the campus already," Eva said, ignoring Alex's crossed eyes. "London's OK, but I much prefer it here." She paused, looking around the Swiss campus, students filling the yard, their noisy chatter rising into the cold air. "There may be sad memories here," Sam knew she was thinking of Pi, "but now there'll be lots of happy ones too."

"Agreed," Sam said, hugging her.

"Your interview all done, Sam?" the Professor called out from across the courtyard.

"Yep," Sam replied, the three of them walking over to join him. "Nora went easy on me, I knew she would. But I know there'll be more to do. Just not today. How did you get on at the UN? Everyone behaving themselves with the Dream Gate, playing nicely?"

"Aha, quite so," the Professor laughed. "It is a bit like that, but fortunately the UN taking control of the site has gone remarkably smoothly. I have high hopes for the excavation of the global treasures and the library. Although these things take time—it will be months before it can all be brought back up. But now that the water has receded, they no longer have to use the long tunnel exit we found in the library, and their work can begin in earnest."

"And Dr. Dark and his men?" Eva asked nervously.

"Still not found," the Professor said. "Unfortunately we may never fully know the extent of Dr. Dark's treachery but it's clear now that he was pulling the strings from afar from the beginning. Stella was probably not aware of his role in it all and Matrix continues to deny all knowledge."

"I hope he's enjoying prison," Alex said, a dark look in his eye. He'd never quite forgotten Matrix's explosive wristbands. He and Shiva had barely escaped with their lives.

"So many unanswered questions," Sam said. "But I'm not sure I really want to hear the answers anyway." He sighed and looked at the Professor.

Does he want to know more about why Sebastian did what he did, or is it better to not know?

"Your face gives you away, Sam," the Professor chided him. "You're thinking about Sebastian—about how he became Solaris."

Sam flushed. "Sorry, Professor."

"Don't be," he replied. "I have the same mixture of curiosity and revulsion about it. Did Sebastian somehow eject from the jet in New York? Or else how did he survive the crash? And just how did he and Dr. Dark come together?"

"At least we know why Solaris always wore a mask," Sam said. "So Sebastian could hide his identity all that time by taking on the disguise of the mythical enemy from the prophecy."

"I've no doubt Sebastian at first used the idea of Solaris to stay hidden," the Professor said, "but even he could not have known that it would ultimately be his destiny to be the incarnation of Solaris, to be the last Dreamer and complete the last 13. As the light rose up to claim the Dream Gate, so the darkness rose up to fight against it." It was the Professor's turn to sigh.

"Hey!" A voice rang out. It was Xavier, running up to join them. "What'd I miss?"

"Not much," Eva laughed, grabbing his arm. "But where's Lora, I thought you were having a tutorial with her?"

"I was, but I begged off early," Xavier said. "Jedi has some new toys to show me. So if you don't need me, I'm outta here!" He ran off again, throwing back a wave as he went.

"I can't believe that guy," Alex said. "Everything he's been through and he's the busiest kid on campus."

"People cope with grief in many ways, Alex," the Professor said. "Don't mistake his actions for indifference.

His life as he knew it shattered that night at the Dream Gate. He's done well to pick himself back up."

"You're right," Alex said, "of course, you're right. I'm just jealous . . . all the girls love him!"

Eva punched his arm. "Whatever," she laughed. "So, Sam, when are you going for another visit to see your family? Maybe I can come with you and see mine too."

Sam thought about his mom and dad, and his corny little brother, Ben. The reunion with them had been awkward but it brought such relief to discover that they were his real parents after all, as well as being Agents. It had been hard on them too, watching from afar as Sam struggled with the prophecy, knowing that to reach out to him would risk putting him, and Ben, in more danger. His relief had been shared by Eva when she discovered her parents had been in the same situation. The video message she'd received had been a cruel ruse by Matrix, using digital images of her parents to trick her. But it would be a long road back, there was a lot of trust to be regained.

But we'll get there. We have all the time in the world now.

"We'll do that soon," Sam said, turning his attention back to Eva.

"Maybe we can all hang out at—" Alex was cut off by a loud whirring noise beyond the courtyard. A loudspeaker crackled. "Could Sam, Alex and Eva please come out to play?"

They turned to look at the Professor. "Go, go on." He